DRAGON THUNDER

DRAGON DREAMER BOOK III

J. S. Burke

LIND PRESS

Athens, Georgia

This is a work of fiction. Names, characters, places, and incidents either are products of the author's imagination or are used fictitiously. Any resemblance to real people, living or dead, or to actual events or places, is entirely coincidental.

Lind Press: www.LINDPRESS.com

Author Site: www.JENNYSBURKE.com

Dedicated to everyone who visits the
Dragon Dreamer worlds.

ACKNOWLEDGMENTS

For helpful insights and suggestions, thanks to Barbara, Chris, Diana, Janice, Jenn, Lisa, Melissa, Tommie, and Roger. I'm very grateful to my editors, Carol and Roger. Thank you to Lind Press. Thanks to all of you who helped in the dragon and undersea worlds!

How many dragons?

BOOKS by J.S. BURKE

THE DRAGON DREAMER

DRAGON LIGHTNING

DRAGON THUNDER

CRYSTAL GEOMETRY

CRYSTAL COLORS

FANTASY SNOWFLAKES COLORING BOOK

Dragon Dreamer Awards

THE DRAGON DREAMER

    *IAN First Place for Best First Novel

    *IAN Finalist for Best Science Fiction

DRAGON LIGHTNING

    *Pinnacle First Place for Best Science Fantasy

    *IAN First Place for Best Science Fiction

CHARACTERS

ICE DRAGON

Cranart – Young dragon-lord, third-in-command.

Drakor – Young dragon-lord who defeated Mardor.

Jardor – Drakor's best friend, his second-in-command.

Jordana – Dragonlet who traveled with golden dragons.

Mardor – Giant dragon-lord and former, long-time ruler.

Merika – Young dragon-lady, friend of Drakor.

Tenira – Older dragon-dam, fourth-in-command.

Zardan – Drakor's sire, crippled in an avalanche.

GOLDEN DRAGON

Arak – Dragon-lord, once bullied as a "Dreamer", now
respected. Drakor's friend, kindred spirit of Scree.

Dorali – Nearly killed as dragonlet, now a scarred Healer.

Karoon – Former bully of Arak, now Dorali's suitor.

Taron – Carver of flutes, builder of ships, Arak's friend.

OCTOPUS

Orm – Scree's mate, gifted scientist and artist.

Scree – Gifted Healer, fearless fighter, friend of dragons.

Scrim – Scree's fosterling, wounded Healer.

Stur – Octopus pod leader, former fosterling of Scree.

CONTENTS

CHAPTER 1: DRAGON THUNDER

The stunted trees cast long, twisted shadows in the evening light. Drakor crouched low at the edge of the field, tasting the wind, tracking his invisible prey. Dew sparkled on tall, feathery grasses as they swayed, marking the path of an unseen creature.

The white dragon dug his claws into the ground. His muscles tensed, ready to spring. Suddenly, his head snapped up.

Drakor stared into the east, into the growing darkness. He leapt into the sky, pumping his wings hard, climbing straight up. Soon the air was so cold that his breath froze. His eyes burned, straining to see past the horizon. But his home was too far away, and now it was gone.

Drakor folded his long, white wings and dove straight down, hurtling through the sky like a star-stone. He snapped his wings wide just in time, raising a thick cloud of dust as he landed. His diamond-shaped scales gleamed like white opal, with a hint of hidden colors and a glittering edge. He was young and still growing, only fourteen feet long from head to tail. But his gray eyes seemed older than his youthful size.

He was the leader of ice dragons.

A white dragon landed beside Drakor and bowed respectfully. "The magnetic lines glowed like the sun, just for an instant. That flash nearly blinded my inner eye! Was that the end?"

Drakor nodded to Jardor, his second-in-command. "Check the magnetic field. Only something major could change it so much." His tail drooped to the ground. "In my vision, our Volcano erupted like never before. A burning tower punched a hole through the clouds, reaching for the stars. Then our island home was gone. It seems like forever since I saw this in my mind, and I have feared it ever since."

Jardor shuddered. "I trusted your vision, but still I hoped you were wrong. It isss hard to accept that our home isss gone." He stared to the east. "Maybe our Volcano will reach the stars and warm our ancestors beside their star-fires."

Drakor flicked his tail uneasily. "Maybe. It gave much energy to *this* world. Sea and sky will use the energy. Giant waves will smash into the shore, but we should be far enough inland. Then the storm will strike.

2

Warn everyone to take shelter. I do not want the dragonlets blown away."

Jardor left to sound the signal drum.

Drakor gazed into the west, where cheerful layers of pink and violet colored the horizon. Night-blooming flowers began to open, adding new scents to the cooling air; the powerful aromas nearly overwhelmed his senses.

His eyes were drawn back to the dark eastern sky, and he shuddered. His home was gone forever, and it felt as if the sun had been ripped from the sky. Drakor turned away from the darkness and flew to the meeting circle, to warn the clan of the coming storm.

Two hours later, a primal scream sounded from across the sea. Black clouds rolled in with electric energy so strong Drakor thought his scales would glow. The stars and moon disappeared, swallowed up by the roiling darkness.

Then the storm struck, fierce beyond anything in their legends.

The wind howled as it ripped off branches and tore trees from the ground. Lightning flashed through the darkness and thunder boomed across the sky. This was Dragon Thunder, the voice of the First Dragon.

*   *   *

BRRRROOOOMMMMM! Scree shuddered as rumbling, thunderous roars tore through her body like the barbs of sting rays. The small octopus gazed east, toward the explosions.

Two volcanoes had erupted, theirs and another to the northeast. Disturbing changes near their undersea home foretold an eruption, warning them to flee.

The second volcano was a lonely island, the ancestral

home of ice dragons. Her friend Drakor had foreseen this eruption, and the stars in his vision showed when it would happen. Scree had learned that their volcanoes were connected, so everyone was in danger.

She stretched each of her eight weary, anxious arms. Beneath her skiff, powerful death waves were already tearing across the sea. And a ferocious storm was coming.

Scree smoothed her skin and removed the gray tinge of worry. Now she was her normal, reddish-brown color, appearing calm and confident. She raised three signal flags on her mast: Tie everything down! Shorten the skiff-wing! Release the bamboo fins!

The other skiff-flyers swiftly complied.

Scree nodded approval. She was leading a fleet of pod-mates into the west, fleeing the destruction of their undersea village. Most items were already tied down. It was standard procedure to shorten the skiff-wing, so it wouldn't be ripped to shreds by fierce storm winds. The bamboo fins were new, her latest invention. Would this help them survive the coming storm?

All too soon, the evening sky changed to an eerie, rusty black. Scree flexed her arms, feeling the cool, damp air. Waves grew taller, washing across the deck and clawing up the mast. The towering peaks became liquid mountains, hiding the other skiffs.

Scree curled her arms nervously. The travelers were still days away from their new home, and the skiffs were dangerously overloaded with last-minute passengers. Could the small skiffs survive this storm?

* * *

Hail pounded Drakor's village. Huge hailstones bounced across the rocky ground like a horde of crystal crickets.

The ice glowed like a thousand eyes in the flashes of lightning. Then rain fell in cold, drenching sheets.

Lightning slashed across the dark clouds. Thunder crackled and boomed. The storm raged through the night while dragons hunkered down in their unfinished dens.

Drakor crouched miserably on the cold, wet floor. His den had a narrow entrance and a circular stone wall that was nearly his height. This blocked the wind, but the incomplete roof did nothing to stop the deluge. He huddled beneath his rough blanket, woven from strips of hemp. But this leaked, too. Relentless, freezing rain slithered through the uneven weave.

If only there had been time to finish his roof! But he used that time to help finish the homes where dragonlets lived with their dams.

An endless crackle of lightning lit his bedraggled den, showing a trough of seawater. Long, slender branches lay soaking in the salty water, to soften and preserve them. A pile of descaled fish skins had been rubbed with grease to make them cloudy-clear. Soon, he would bend the branches into a tall, arched frame and cover it with the skins.

A proper roof gave shelter, but it was also a cloudy window to the sky. He would watch glowing sunsets and swirling auroras through this ceiling. Ice dragons needed the sky as a fish needs water.

Drakor shook water out of his eyes as he gazed up into the flashing darkness. He sighed and curled up tight, trying to sleep through the thunderous shaking and icy torrents of rain.

* * *

Drakor woke at dawn to a deathly silence. That ferocious

storm had finally died. He tossed off his sodden blanket, shook out the sparkling storm ice, and chewed chunks of smoked redfish. Then he ate clawfulls of walnuts mixed with dried cranberries, his new favorite combination. These tart red berries were an unexpected treasure, discovered in a nearby bog.

Drakor left his den and filled his lungs with the cool spring air. He instinctively looked east. Would their Volcano truly join the after-world? Would it warm past dragons beside their star-fires in the sky? Would his dam feel this warmth? A comforting lullaby played in his mind, a rare memory from the brief time before she left him.

Drakor strode through the village, checking each den, asking questions. He breathed a sigh of relief. Everyone had survived that ferocious storm.

The young leader gazed to the west, where morning mist rose from between the hills like dragon's breath. Drakor stretched his wings, feeling the freedom of the wind and the pull of the unknown. He forced his wings back into stiff folds. Soon, he promised his inner dragon. But his feet kept walking, closer and closer to those hills.

Jardor, his second-in-command, landed beside him. "This world isss bigger than I could have imagined. The fishing isss great! But our new Volcano does not speak or warm the ground. I miss the rumbling on our island home. I even miss that awful smell."

Drakor nodded. Their island was home for countless generations of ice dragons. It had biting winds, black Volcano grit, and the eternal stench of rotten eggs. They were often hungry. How could he miss it so much? "Nothing could ever replace our home, but this place isss a good match." His ears twitched at the whine of mosquitoes. "And it definitely has the same annoying insects."

Their new village lay between two lakes. Light glinted off the huge lake to the south, which was home to tasty red fish half as long as Drakor. The close lake, to the north, was small and shallow. This should freeze well for their winter games. Northwest of the village, a glacier ground across the land, groaning and dropping boulders.

Jardor gazed to the east with a wistful expression. "Some dragons say that our island home isss still there."

Drakor shook his head. "That isss just wishful thinking and lies spread by Mardor. Clan legends give the warning signs. The shift in the magnetic field and that terrible storm show that our old home isss gone."

He stretched his cramped wings. "Some dragons ignore all the signs. They need to see to believe. But seeing the empty place of our lost island would bring them no joy."

Drakor fell silent, flicking his tail up and down, up and down. He was sure his good friend Arak had a unique, secret gift. That golden dragon could do more than just share thoughts while in trance-mind. He must be able to see what was really there when he mind-traveled. And he would find empty sea where their island had lived.

Drakor sighed. He owed everything to Arak: his life, his wings, even his victory and the survival of his clan. So he would never ask his friend about his secret.

A dragon's claws clicked sharply on the stones.

Drakor's head whipped around as he was startled from his thoughts.

Jardor looked him in the eye. "The leader should check on the storage pit."

Drakor nodded and followed him to the middle of their new village. This was the best place to protect their crucial supplies. Before the storm, he had covered the pit with fish skins to keep out the rain. Now, two dragons worked on opposite sides, straining against ropes as they hauled up buckets of dirt.

Drakor stepped to the edge and peered down, to where dragon-lords dug deeper into the shadows. "This isss deep enough. Pave the floor with river stones."

A huge dragon grumbled loudly, "We left our storage pit with all of our wonderful food." He balanced a heavy bucket of dirt on each massive shoulder and stomped past Drakor, ignoring the young leader.

Drakor ground his teeth. He should demand respect, but what if the dragon did *not* back down? This dragon had been Mardor's second-in-command. What if this dragon challenged him to a leadership fight . . . and he lost?

Jardor stared after the dragon. "He remembers food we never had. We were practically starving on our island."

Drakor clicked his claws together. "His memory isss quite flexible, but his mind isss not. He changes the past to suit him, but he cannot imagine *me* as the new leader."

He turned his head and found Mardor staring at him. That giant could not imagine any world where *he* was not the leader. And he wanted his power back.

8

CHAPTER 2: DEATH WAVE

Drakor took a deep breath, tasting the cool breeze, noting scents of smoke and fish. Then a group of dragon-dams walked by, grumbling just loud enough to be overheard. "Starting the same work here that we *just finished* on our island."

Jardor raised an eye ridge. "What work?"

Drakor nodded toward the meadow. "Digging more tubers. We need more of everything: cranberries from the bog, dried grapes, acorns, walnuts, and pine nuts. Herbs for tea and roots for that Sassafras drink. And, if we find that bee hive, we can store honey in gemstone jars."

Five young dragons touched down in a perfect ring around him, smiling at their precision landing. One opened her lumpy sack, releasing a pleasant, earthy aroma. "We hunted in the foothills. These are the best mushrooms I ever tasted!"

Drakor grinned. These dragons were his size, his age-mates, and they often found the best new foods for their evening gatherings. It helped to hear dragons speak of what they *liked* here. Then his ears twitched at a new noise.

Three small dragonlets began jumping up and down on sacks, laughing hysterically. One poured a sack of crushed pinecones onto the blanket. Then all three raked with their claws, hunting through the debris. They tossed pine nuts into a bucket, counting points for hitting the center or pinging off the inside wall.

Drakor smiled. "Clever youngsters. They make a game of getting nuts from those old, broken cones. Pine nuts will be as valued as gemstones when everyone isss tired of fish."

He looked up as the ground shook, rumbling like a Volcano.

A giant dragon stomped by with a huge fish slung over one shoulder. He turned and stared at the leader while flexing his sharp claws.

Drakor noted the claws; it looked as if the dragon was mentally shredding him into tiny pieces. He locked eyes with Mardor until the larger dragon lowered his gaze. The giant turned and stalked away from the new leader.

Drakor shivered. He was too young, too small, and yet he beat Mardor in the challenge fight. Then he took the clan away from a home they loved and a doom they never saw. Now he was an upstart leader in a new land facing unknown dangers.

Jardor looked from Mardor to Drakor. "He really hates you."

Drakor nodded. "Mardor would not listen to reason, so I challenged him."

Jardor clapped him on the shoulder. "And you won. Every dragon survived the long flight here, except for one old dragon-lord. He refused to travel on Arak's skiff."

Drakor took a deep, slow breath, noting all the unknown scents. They were still strangers in a new land. "I became leader so the clan could escape the death of our home. But the clan never saw our Volcano explode."

Drakor sighed. "Many believe our island isss still there. They think we left a perfectly good home and endured a brutal move for no reason. To survive *here*, I need the support of all the dragons, and especially Mardor. The clan must work together."

He studied the growing storm clouds. "Legend says that this coming winter will be long and harsh. Can we store enough food to survive, with enough kinds to stay healthy? Can we learn the ways of our New World before winter closes in?"

Drakor clicked his claws together. The dwire were another problem. These large predators could camouflage nearly as well as his octopus friend Scree.

How could they defend against invisible killers?

* * *

Scree woke at dawn as the water lightened around her. She curled and uncurled each of her eight intelligent arms, stretching. Then she tasted the sea with her sensitive suckers. A cool current flowed past her cave, bringing new flavors of life and death, and she stored this information in her main brain.

Bright orange fish darted through the reef like frantic butterflies, while moonstone jellyfish pulsed slowly above. Scree smiled. These ocean clouds held needles of death, but no lightning storms. She felt the gritty sand outside her cave, sensed movement below the surface, and pounced. She made a quick snack of the cherry clam.

Her new home was hidden beneath furry branches of coral trees. The volcano near her old home had awakened, rumbling and shaking, bleeding toxic new flavors into the sea. So the entire pod fled across the sea in a fleet of small skiffs, leaving their village and almost everything else behind.

They left just in time.

An explosion shattered the sky. Then the storm struck. Monstrous waves attacked the skiffs with curling white claws, grabbing the sides. A normal skiff would have been dragged under.

But Scree was ready.

At her signal, bamboo rafts rolled out from the sides of each skiff. These huge fins spread across the water and merged with the waves. The skiffs no longer fought the sea. They became the sea.

Scree had surfed the waves, jetted through coral forests, even rode a few sharks. But nothing felt quite like this, with a terror and excitement beyond any experience. It was the best ride ever!

Scree eyed the bare rock walls of her new cave. There were no glowing tapestries. The shelves weren't up, and the ceiling had holes. She peered outside. The sand was not yet paved with colorful shells and pebbles. Worse, there was no medicinal garden.

Scree pulsed a sigh, then straightened her arms. It was time to get to work. She planted clumps of long, feathery, red seaweed that swayed with the currents, adding color and movement to her Healer garden. She fastened two long shelves along the wall. Then she pulsed to the roof of her cave and fitted rocks into the largest holes.

Scree pulled on the clear glass bars across the entrance, testing. They held. This was a barrier to curious reef residents, a protective screen she could see through and squeeze through. The bars were lightning casts, a gift from her dragon friend Arak. He rode the storm, making lightning strikes on the beach, which melted a path of glass through the sand.

Scree left her cave and pulsed through the reef. She passed a cluster of lively flowers eating a dead fish. These lemon yellow anemones were rooted to the stone, catching and killing with their poisonous petals. When food became scarce, the flowers could glide away to a better place.

Scree twirled her anxious arms, thinking. Had she chosen a good place for the pod to move?

The coral forest cast a dark web of shadows across the sand, like the orb of a monstrous spider. Scree held still, feeling the sounds, flavors, and motions of the sea, checking for danger. A new taste seeped into the sea. She glided toward the unexpected flavor, moving like a shadow.

Suddenly, right beside her, a coral rock shape-shifted into an octopus. She signed to her mate, weaving words with two of her flexible arms. "Orm! Your camouflage was perfect."

He grinned. "This crab thought so, too. It got too close, and now we have dinner." He held the stone crab by its huge claws while pushing down and in. Both claws dropped off the crab, like dead leaves from a winter tree. The crab scuttled away.

Orm dropped the claws into his pouch. "The crab will grow new ones. What made you think of adding bamboo fins to our skiffs?"

Scree turned happy-green. "Remember when Arak's bamboo raft carried an injured dragon to the skiff? It flexed with the waves. That sparked an idea. I designed bamboo fins to flex with storm waves, to help the skiffs. The dragons finished making them just in time."

Orm changed his skin color to match her green. "Clever. We're lucky, too. That storm carried us here faster than expected. It's so good to be back on shifting sand, instead of those roiling waves! But I feel a disturbing flavor. Is it from a sleepy volcano? Or something worse?"

Scree nodded. "I feel/taste this, too. I wish Drakor could dream up the answer." She looked northwest. "He must have his claws full, trying to lead those ice dragons. Especially Mardor."

*   *   *

Drakor landed on the hilltop, where the wind blew strongest. He leaned into the wind, feeling the freedom. A flare of energy glowed in his mind, drawing his eyes to the ground. Small, glassy-green stones lay scattered among the dull gray rocks. Zircon! Green was a rare color for this gemstone. Why did it look like a stormy sea, feel

14

like melted sand, and have such intense inner energy?

Drakor clicked his claws together. These acorn-sized gems could be used as secret guard stones, dropped into the storage pits as they were filled. After the pits were sealed, he would feel if anything inside was moved. There might be tunneling creatures who could steal from below or, worse, even a rogue dragon. To survive, the clan needed everything they could store, and more.

Drakor searched the ground, gathering every green stone he could find. An hour later he found no more of the green zircon rocks, just a few blue. He stored the sparkling, sky-blue zircon in another pouch.

Drakor flew back, landing beside Jardor. His nostrils flared at the powerful aromas.

Jardor wrinkled his nose. "We caught enough fish to fill *both* smoke boxes. I wish I liked smoked fish."

Drakor grinned. "I hated it too, at first. Now the smoky flavors seem dragonny." He took two heavy, golden crystals from his pouch and tossed them to Jardor. "I found more strike-stones! These are for you. This isss a safer way to start a fire than with lightning strikes."

Jardor dropped the bright stones into his pouch. "Thanks! New World fires are great, but why must we make so much smoked fish? Dried fish taste better. Even pickled fish taste better!"

Drakor clicked his claws together. "Smoked fish will last better than dried fish, and there are not enough jars for pickled fish. The clan cannot afford to lose any of our stored food. The world will change because our Volcano exploded."

Jardor snapped his tail in dismay. "We lost our home. What could be worse?"

Drakor gazed east, toward the unseen sea. "We do not often share our most ancient legends. Many say these things never happened. Some call them the Lost Legends, made up by a dragon who lost his mind. But my sire taught me all the legends, and he believes these are true."

Drakor flicked his tail up and down. His eyes glazed over, as if in a trance. "A Volcano exploded and destroyed a long-ago home of ice dragons. Everyone died except for the dragons who were away, fishing. Sunsets were fiery red and orange, like a bleeding Volcano. Winter was so cold that the sea waves were thick and frosty, moving like slush snow. That winter was long, lasting many seasons, until there was no food left. Most of the dragons died."

Jardor shuddered. "Yes, that isss worse."

Drakor caught the glint of silver on a dragon's wingtips. "Jardor, that dragon-lady isss with egg! Where should she nest?"

Jardor frowned. "Somewhere safe and warm?"

Drakor flicked his tail nervously. "That isss a problem. Safe isss easier than warm. But now we should check the forest."

Drakor landed at the edge and his eyes grew wide. The ground was littered with branches, leaves, flowers, and vines torn off by the wind. Beams of light shone through new holes in the forest, where uprooted giants had crashed down.

Jardor poked at pale flower tassels and big maroon blossoms. "This means no fall harvest of nuts, golden Paw-Paws, or grapes."

Drakor's wings drooped as he stared at the forest of destruction. "No mulberries or black cherries, and Arak said those are the best. Our harvest was stolen by the storm. Weather isss more dangerous than Mardor."

He straightened his wings. "Fish may survive in the deep lake, but dragons need more than fish. I hope we can harvest the sea for clams and seaweed."

Drakor looked southeast, toward the distant sea. Scree had moved there with her pod. The last he heard, she was skiff-flying through that fierce storm. How was she?

* * *

Coral shadows stretched longer and darker as Scree flowed across the reef, checking with all her senses. The sea still tasted odd, and now it was vibrating to a dangerous beat. Why?

A frilly, purple-and-rose sea slug danced in the water. Yellow spikes ran down its back, each tipped with a tiny blue eye. Quithra! Where would it go to spawn? She needed the eggs to make a numbing salve for aching arms, which was popular with older octopi.

Suddenly, a sea current brushed her skin. Scree spun around with her arms out, stiff, ready to fight or jet away. Then her body went limp with relief. She signed to her mate, "Would you like to hunt?"

Orm nodded. "Where?"

Scree pointed toward the undersea canyon, where a sheer wall dropped into eternal darkness. "We haven't hunted there."

Orm shook his head. "That's where the sharks hunt."

Scree grinned. "We could catch another ride." She concentrated on the millions of cells in her red-brown skin, changing the color of each cell. In an instant, a vivid picture appeared: an octopus rode a shark through the blue-green sea.

Orm rolled his eyes. "You may enjoy shark rides, but I had enough excitement on the trip here. We're still learning the ways of our new reef. Let's hunt closer to home."

Moonbeams filtered down through the sea, adding a silvery light. Turquoise anemones waved their glowing petals. She pointed to small, white eggs that gleamed in the dark water, like stars in the night sky. "Those must be from reef fish, the ones that stay here. Are the migrating fish doing as well?"

Scree and Orm pulsed through coral branches, following a trail of subtle sounds and flavors. She peered into a crevice. Something glimmered in the shadows and she froze. An iridescent lobster! It caught all the light, shining like precious white opal.

Scree signed, "That's too rare to eat. Let's keep hunting." She pointed. "Orm, look!" Cold water flowed across her sensitive skin as she squirted down.

Orm gazed at the brown sand dollars with a dreamy expression. "They're like that stack of chocolate cookies Zarina made. Dragons and octopi. Who could have guessed we'd get along so well?"

Scree grinned. "Arak would say you have a sweet tooth."

Orm changed his skin cell colors and covered his body with a simple design. Sharp, white tooth triangles stood out against the dragon-gold. "I do like sweets. I'm glad you met him."

Scree curled an arm beneath her head. "I'd never seen a dragon. Arak had beautiful golden scales, but he was all sharp claws and teeth. When he crashed onto that ice, I wanted to flee back into the sea."

Orm laughed. "You? Choose safety?"

Scree nodded. "He was bigger than a shark! But he was torn and bleeding. I just couldn't let him die, all alone on the floating ice."

Orm reached over and twined arms with his mate. "I know. You're a Healer. Golden dragons can be scary, but ice dragons are as fierce as giant squid!"

Scree tilted her head in a dragonly way, considering. "Yes, they are. I rather like that."

Orm laughed. "Of course you do.

Scree looked north. "Remember the first time we met Drakor? Now he's the leader of ice dragons. That job must be harder than tackling a horde of giant squid!"

Orm shuddered. "Neither job appeals to me."

Scree made pictures of seaweed growing up her body. "A long winter will be worse on land than in the sea. We could grow extra food for the dragons. They may need it."

Orm held still, in his thinking pose. "I'll see what we can manage. Let's hunt, and I'll fix a tasty meal with dragon spices!"

Suddenly, the ocean shuddered. Waves tore through the water, tumbling rocks and ancient coral. Scree was grabbed by the sea, twisted and wrenched, battered and bruised. This was a death wave. Where did it come from?

She tried to peer through the turbulent water. Then a dark cloud of mud covered her like a shroud. Her body went limp, and the light went out of her eyes.

She was buried alive.

CHAPTER 3: SEAQUAKE

At star-rise, Drakor lay tensely coiled in his den. Strange scents crept in from the nearby forest. Suddenly, his silvery, fish-skin pouch turned green with reflected light. He rolled over and gazed up through the partial roof. A sea-green aurora twisted and twirled across the sky.

Drakor gave a deep sigh. This wandering light was much like his thoughts. He sat up and stretched, working the knots out of his muscles. What should he do about Mardor and his angry supporters?

Drakor restlessly drew in the dirt floor, sketching a circle of fire-breathing dragons. This design matched an ornament made by a friend. Golden dragons grew fanciful snowflakes in the winter clouds, put them on pine sap, and zapped to create lacy amber ornaments.

He stared at the drawing, reliving his fierce fight with

Mardor. Then he looked up at the star-studded sky. His dam lived with these star-fires. What would she think of him now? What advice would she have?

Drakor pulled a wood flute from his pouch and fingered the holes. He played a simple tune, quietly, matching the tempo to the dancing aurora. Music flowed through his mind, relaxing him as nothing else could.

Drakor checked the position of the stars. It was time. He tucked the flute back into his pouch and pulled out an ice-clear ball, his quartz trance-stone. Arak had promised to mind-call from across the sea.

Drakor stilled his mind and stared into the center of his clear quartz globe, sinking deeper into trance. The globe seemed to shimmer, glowing from within. Then he was looking down on his limp body. His trance-mind traveled east, toward the shore, drawn to a matching shimmer. As the trance-mind shimmers overlapped, he heard Arak's voice deep within his mind, as if in a cave. The voice was a flat monotone.

Drakor. How was the flight

Arak. We flew longer than I hoped to, but we made it here. All but one. How were the big waves

Even worse than expected

How are the octopi

I have not heard. Scree must be busy

When will you bring our ice dragons to the New World

We leave in three days. Remember the rainbow cave we found. We will stay there

Drakor's trance-mind traveled back to his empty body. He opened his eyes, put the globe back in its pouch, and lay down. The leaves of his bed crackled in a normal, comforting way. His body demanded sleep, but new questions sparked in his mind.

How much had survived the towering tsunamis and fierce storm? Would the entire clan of golden dragons move here? And, would they have food to trade?

The ribbons of light twisted faster now, like dragons surfing a dangerous storm. This aurora was as tangled as his thoughts before he fought Mardor. And as hard as it was to win that terrible challenge fight, leading the clan was harder.

Mardor had ruled with steel claws. Dragons gave him instant obedience. But Drakor was the youngest, smallest leader ever. Some ignored his orders, while a few openly questioned his commands. Soon, a dragon would challenge him.

Could he win again?

*   *   *

Scree jerked back to consciousness. She was buried alive in thick mud. Her body screamed for oxygen, but everywhere felt the same, with no up or down. Which way to the sea? She held still, feeling for any sound in the muffling mud. She felt a faint vibration from the churning sea, but it seemed to come from below! She was all turned around.

Scree pulled arm over arm through the muck, dragging her body toward the distant feel/sound of the angry sea. She must escape before this homing beacon stopped moving.

Finally, her head pushed through into the water. But she still couldn't breathe. Spots danced before her eyes. The world spun darker.

As her main brain faded away, her eight intelligent

arms rallied. They reached up together, squishing mud out of her breathing-gills. Her body drew in a weak pulse of gritty oxygen-water. Then another. Her main brain awoke.

Scree's arms grew stronger. She climbed out of the muck and stared through the cloudy, whirling sea. Where was Orm? The tip of an arm poked up from the thick, gray sludge. He was drowning in mud!

"ORM!"

Scree dug down, grabbed the limp arm, and pulled. A pale, deathly gray octopus emerged from the muck. She wrapped four arms around his head, gently squishing the thick mud out of the tubes to his gills. At last, he could breathe. But nothing happened. He had no pulse!

She squeezed the hearts on either side, beneath his gills. Then she squeezed the third heart, sending renewed blood to his oxygen-starved body.

Orm remained as limp as a jellyfish washed ashore.

She squeezed all three hearts in the proper rhythm, again and again, pumping blood for her mate.

He was still as death.

Scree sent a micro-zap of energy deep into each heart, just as she squeezed them.

His hearts began to beat! Scree's skin pulsed with an odd mix of happy-green and worry colors. Everything was working, but his body didn't even twitch! When would Orm wake up? The minutes dragged on, each with a day's worth of torment. Then, slowly, the normal red-brown color crept back into his gray skin.

The spark of life returned to his eyes, and his limp arms whispered, "Scree."

She sighed. "I *told* you not to do this to me again."

He smiled faintly. "What? Don't almost die, or don't

find my way back?"

Scree twined two arms with her mate and gazed deep into his eyes. "Don't leave me."

Orm reached up feebly and twined a third arm. "Never. That odd vibration was a seaquake warning?"

Scree nodded. "The water's still sloshing around."

Orm grimaced. "Almost dying makes an octopus hungry, but my pouch was torn away." He struggled upright, carefully arranging his shaky arms for support.

Scree reached into her pouch, plucked out four thin-shelled clams, and gave them all to her mate.

Orm hesitated. "That's your emergency food. Aren't you hungry, too?"

Scree shook her head. "This *is* an emergency. You nearly died, and you need *all* this energy to recover. I'll hunt when the sea calms down."

The water grew clearer as the sea stopped churning. Sand, mud, and dead things sank to the seafloor. But the sounds and tastes of the sea still felt odd, all jumbled together.

Scree helped Orm crawl to a huge barrel sponge. It was firmly attached to a rare, solid patch of rock and still standing. "Rest in here. This should be a safe place if there are any more death waves. I'll be right back."

Orm climbed slowly up the side of the sponge, slid down into the curved center, and camouflaged. He turned shiny brown and added shallow holes in his skin, becoming part of the ancient animal.

Scree nodded approval and crawled away, feeling as gray as the sea. She waved her arms through the water, tasting, and followed a death trail to a cream-and-tan calico crab. It was squashed by rocks that must have fallen in the seaquake.

Scree made quick work of this meal, and her color improved as she fed. Then she glided along the sand, feeling the flavors of the sea.

A mantis shrimp lay pinned beneath a rock, leaking clear blue blood. It was about half her length, shaped like a lobster, and painted with all the brilliant reef colors. The long, narrow body had segments of green and teal with an edge of midnight blue. There were eight ruby legs and two powerful, orange claws. The huge, iridescent eyes sparkled like rainbow opals.

Scree slipped forward to end its pain and make a meal. The colorful creature was trapped, nearly dead, but still she approached warily. This ferocious predator had few enemies despite its small size. The striking claws were deadly. Mantis had the fastest punch in the sea!

The mantis stared fearlessly into her eyes and flashed a rapid pattern of light.

Scree blinked. She could barely count the flashes. It was so fast! And there were odd gaps in the message. Was there light she couldn't see?

Using its free claw, the mantis sketched a triangle in the sand. The Healer triangle.

Scree pulsed white with shock and then surprise-pink. A shrimp asking for help? How did it even know how? Scree studied her prey. Her *former* prey. She glanced again. It was male. She moved the rock off the mantis and began healing her unusual patient.

He sketched a picture in the sand of a male mantis tending the eggs.

Scree nodded. Mantis shrimp mated for life and took turns guarding the eggs. This must be his season to tend their nest while his mate hunted.

Then he drew a squashed mantis.

Scree pulsed gray with sorrow. His mate must be dead. She again felt that terrible emptiness from finding Orm buried in the muck, limp and gray, when he nearly died.

She pointed to herself. "Scree." She pointed to him and signed, "What's your name?"

The mantis struck his sturdy claw against the rock, moving so fast she couldn't see! That was an odd experience. An octopus could shape-shift in the blink of an eye, but he moved even faster.

"Strike." The mantis flashed another light pattern, again with gaps.

She stared. He *must* be using light beyond her sight.

He looked right at her and his eye stalks twitched.

Scree could almost read his mind: she was a soft, shell-less creature who could barely see and was too dim-witted to understand. She stiffened at his arrogance and then quivered with laughter. He was a shrimp by nature and size, but accustomed to power and abilities beyond most creatures. And that could be useful.

* * *

Scree jetted back to Orm. She shuddered at his ghostly color and immediately emptied her sack. "Eat. You'll feel better."

Orm devoured the clams. "Thanks. What took so long?"

"I was helping a wounded shrimp."

"Treating? Not eating?"

She laughed as they pulsed home together. "I offered to feed Strike so he can tend his eggs. He's clever, and he can see light that we can't."

Orm stared. "I know that look. What are you planning?"

"Fish and turtles line up at cleaning stations to be rid of parasites. Octopus apprentices help me treat problems beyond parasites, in my Healing Station. What if different beings work together to heal, sharing our unique abilities?"

Orm stopped pulsing. "Like dragons and octopi?"

Scree nodded. "Dragons and turtles see magnetic lines, but we can't. What can a mantis see? Maybe Strike could help me with those strange new tumors that are cropping up." She turned happy-green as they reached their caves. Only a few stones had fallen. But her cheerful green quickly faded to gray. Some of the oldest coral trees had shattered.

Orm sighed. "Many generations of octopi will hatch and pass on, becoming one with the sea, before this coral regrows to its former size."

Scree curled her arms in distress. "And that disturbing sea flavor has grown stronger. What does it mean?"

CHAPTER 4: GHOST SKY

Drakor sighed in relief as he fastened the last translucent fish-skin panel onto his roof. No dragons died in the storm, they caught plenty of fish, and his den was finally finished. Everything was going well. He curled up on his nice, dry bed. The crisp leaves crackled pleasantly beneath him, releasing earthy aromas as he dropped into an easy sleep.

Drakor woke to a rose and violet sunrise glowing through his ceiling. He left his den, grinning as this cheerful dawn became a clear blue sky.

Then a dark shadow crept across the ground.

Drakor stared up at the cloudless sky. His eyes grew wide when the bright morning sky turned a dull, dusky gray. The sun became a pale ghost, as if trapped behind a dark, unseen cloud. Robbed of light, the world had dark, muddy colors. A chill spread through the air.

Dragons flicked their tails nervously as they worked, whispering about strange omens in this strange land. Why did they have to move? And why did they move *here*?

Drakor moved from group to group, reminding them of their ancient legends. These were the changes to expect after an eruption destroyed their island. But many did not believe their island was gone.

The perpetual twilight weighed them down, and discontent grew with each unnatural day.

Drakor was burdened by the odd gray sky and constant grumbling. Night after night, he barely slept. He woke slowly on the fourth day, craving sleep. He squinted at the sunrise that shone through his ceiling. Light! After three days of eerie twilight, this was a welcome change. He opened both eyes. Then he stared.

The ceiling glowed in curious shades of green.

Drakor bolted from his den. Green skies warned of fierce storms with monstrous hail, or deadly tornadoes. He scanned the sky, searching in every direction. Where were the dangerous thunderclouds?

Dragons crowded together, eyes wide, staring. The sky was green, with *no* clouds! Then a glowing green ball rose up into the sky.

A youngster squeaked, "The sun isss *green!*"

Drakor snapped his tail, as surprised as the others. Green skies were not even mentioned in the legends.

29

A dragon-lord shouted, "This isss a warning!"

Drakor clicked his claws together, thinking. The clan was unsettled by the move, but this was worse, something completely unexpected. Still, the green sky *must* be caused by their Volcano. He stood taller, moved to the center of the crowd, and raised his wings high.

For once, the dragons fell silent, waiting for him to speak. But what could he say?

Drakor gazed at the sky, which nearly matched the grass . . . "Green isss the color of spring, the time to celebrate new hatchings. Our Volcano sends us green skies to celebrate our new beginnings here, as he travels to join the stars."

A dragon muttered, "Maybe our Volcano isss sending us a warning to leave this place."

Mardor muscled his way to Drakor and stretched even taller, standing well above the crowd. "This isss our island calling us home."

Drakor gritted his teeth and ignored Mardor, as if this claim was not worth a reply. If only he could prove that their island was gone! He glanced east, recalling their last meal before they left their island. "Tonight we will feast to celebrate our new home and this sign of approval from our Volcano."

A dragon began thumping her tail. Friends joined in, cheerfully pounding the ground, drowning out the protests.

Drakor assigned dragons to help with the feast. Then the crowd trickled away.

The sun and sky remained green the entire day. Dragons spent most of the day staring at the sky, so the only thing they finished was their feast.

That evening, a vivid green sunset wrapped the world in this unexpected color. Drakor stood still, watching. Then he snapped his tail. Even the moon and stars were green! It was unbelievably beautiful and equally disturbing, like living inside a mythical globe. If this strange sky was from a dying Volcano, what would their after-home be like?

Drakor was stiff with worry. He tried to identify each green in this odd, intangible world and then match it with the real world. There were gemstone shades of intense emerald, pale peridot, cloudy jade, sparkling green opal, and more. He found the greens of iridescent beetles, mushrooms, ferns, and tree leaves. Maybe this alien green world was not so different from theirs. His wings began to relax. But the next day, the sky glowed in shades of green he had never seen!

Drakor walked by a surly group of ice dragons. These were Mardor's followers, the biggest dragons in the clan, and they all wanted him to fail.

Mardor snapped his long tail. "This isss not spring green. It isss green like the mold on old dead things."

Mardor's former second-in-command growled, "It isss green like the mist from a poisonous mushroom."

Drakor stared them down but, if they were not challenging his leadership, he would have laughed. It was clever. Mardor was more than a fierce mountain of muscle, and this made him even more dangerous.

For three days and nights they lived in a glowing green world. Then, on the fourth day, their normal yellow sun returned. These unnerving greens disappeared, and the cloudless afternoon sky was blue.

Drakor breathed a deep sigh of relief.

Sunrise and sunset glowed brighter than ever, but only in fiery reds and orange. There were no purples, pinks, or greens. When the sun rose and set, flaming colors filled the sky, as if the entire world was a Volcano burning.

*   *   *

Afternoon light slanted through the sea as Scree headed for the canyon, and beyond. She pulsed just above the coral, automatically searching for Healer supplies. Her main brain focused through thousands of tiny eyes in her skin, gathering a wider picture of the reef.

She swooped down to collect slime from the mustard-yellow fronds of a soft coral. This goo helped fight infections.

Scree tasted the currents as she traveled, checking with the sensitive suckers in her arms. Both of the eastern volcanoes leaked chemicals before they exploded. Death waves had raced across the sea, carrying rotting carcasses, floating rocks, and odd chemicals. And the latest wave, the one that nearly killed Orm, carried new problems.

The reef was changing. There weren't as many migrating fish. Turtles were growing tumors. And what was happening in the abyss, in the home of the giant squid? They had attacked the pod twice in their old village. She negotiated a treaty but, if fish died off, these hungry giants could attack again.

Scree stopped at the edge of the reef, where pink algae made a bright, wrinkled crust on the rocks. She peered into the abyss. The living reef continued down the canyon wall, with feathery red worms, blue anemone flowers, and knobby purple sponges. She pushed off into the cold, strong current. It was like flying in a wild winter storm!

Scree twirled down into the twilight zone. Corals and seaweed disappeared with the fading light, replaced by sponges, anemones, and ancient life. She felt very few fish songs and caught no glimmer of scales. Where were the fish? Had they died? Moved away? Or were they just hiding?

Scree gazed down into the deep abyss, where odd glowing creatures lit the eternal darkness like stars. She wore a ring of glowing anemones around her mantle and carried food to attract glowfish. This living light would help her explore. She took a long pulse of oxygen-water. It was time to dive deep.

A huge shadow slid across the sea like a dark cloud.

Scree looked up and stared. This shark was as big as a giant squid!

The monster angled down and swam right at her.

It was too late to camouflage.

Scree held her arms out, stiff and steady, waiting calmly to defend while the eye-skin behind her head searched frantically for a crevice to hide. Squirting ink would be a last-minute distraction, a cloud to hide behind while she jetted away.

The shark tilted sideways, and her anxious arms went limp with relief. There were white dots across its broad back. This was a whale shark, a gentle giant.

The shark stopped right beside Scree. What did it want? Then her sensitive arms curled away at the terrible feel/taste of rotted flesh. A long rope was wrapped tightly around the base of its huge tail fin.

Scree flushed gray with worry. She grabbed the sharpest blade in her Healer bag, a red-and-blue knife.

This was made from a ruby-and-sapphire gemstone; only diamond was harder. Drakor had carved this gift in thanks, after she helped put his shattered wing back together.

Scree slid her knife under the rope and sawed upward. Half fell away, but the remaining rope was stuck in the cut. The shark flinched but held still while she tugged the rope out of the wound. Then she pushed iodine-rich seaweed into the deep cut, to kill infection.

Scree took a closer look at the rope, which was woven from an unknown plant. Golden dragons made braided ropes from strips of fish skin. Ice dragons wove ropes from hemp. So who made *this* rope? The sunset dragons? And where was the shark when he got tangled up in the rope?

Scree patted the shark's rough, sandpaper skin and pulsed away. The giant fish turned and nudged her gently, wriggling his body. She turned surprise-pink at the invitation. Scree settled on the shark's back and fastened her suckers to its scales. He swam off, faster and faster. This was more fun than riding a wave to shore! Then the shark circled back, returning her to the place where they met.

Scree slipped off. She gazed into his eye, and understanding passed between them. It could be helpful to have such a large friend, and whale sharks had long memories.

Evening shadows stretched longer, telling the time. Part-way home she met Orm, curling his arms with concern.

"It's late. Where were you?"

Scree turned happy-green. "Riding a shark. You're

right, that cliff at the edge of darkness is the perfect place to find them! Orm, I need your help. You can identify chemicals just by tasting the sea, better than anyone else."

Scree looked toward the mysterious edge. "We need to visit the abyss. You can check chemicals while I check fish songs. Then we'll know what's happening here, what types of fish remain, and how many. If there aren't enough fish after those eruptions, giant squid may start hunting us again."

Orm stretched his arms while his skin pulsed with shadowy-gray images.

Scree watched this blurry skin-movie. What was he thinking?

Then he rolled his eyes. "You think the promise of a shark ride will make me want to help?"

Scree twined two arms with her mate. "No. You'll come for the chemistry."

He grinned. "Ours? Or the sea?"

She twined a third arm and pulled him closer. "Both." Then she flexed her arms nervously. "We must find the source of the problem. Everything is connected, so this could harm octopi *and* dragons."

CHAPTER 5: SPARKLING MENACE

Drakor stretched his long, leathery wings, soaking up the sun. The first storage pit was now stocked with food and a few of his secret guard stones. This cloudless sky promised a perfect day for digging the next pit.

Suddenly, the sky turned gray. Thin, silvery lines danced before his inner eye, like sparkling spider webs. Ice energy! Drakor whistled a warning and raced to his den. He shivered as the temperature dropped faster than a falling star-stone. Then hail rained down, thick and furious.

Drakor nearly stepped on a mantis in his den. The insect spread its glossy wings in a threat display, gleaming like ice. This fierce hunter was no longer than his claw, a sparkling menace as dangerous to insects as this glittering storm was to dragons.

An hour later, the hailstorm simply stopped. The sky turned bright blue, as if it had never held a cloud.

Dragons crawled out of their shelters. A few were bleeding and the rest must be bruised. They crowded together, flexing wings and snapping tails, staring. Ice balls sparkled across the ground like a cold, pebbly beach.

One dragon poked the ground. "This ice must be three feet thick!"

Another stared at the sky. "What a freaky storm! It came with no warning."

Drakor walked to the center of the crowd, treading carefully on the slippery, sparkling crystals. The last thing he needed was to fall flat on his face in front of the clan! He raised his wings and waited. For once, he was glad that they took so long to settle down. He needed that time to think. This unpredictable weather was a menace that nobody could fight. What could he say to calm their fears?

An old dragon-lord with silvered scales raised his wing. "In all my years, I have never seen so much ice! Why isss the weather so strange here?"

Drakor spread his arms wide, palms down, in a calming gesture. "Our Volcano exploded. Legends tell us that weather changes *everywhere* when this happens. The sky will calm down in a few years."

"Years?"

Drakor shared a confident smile. "Yes. Our Volcano

37

isss sending us new memories as it leaves for the stars. We will see the world as we never have before, and have interesting stories to tell future hatchlings! Today isss a holiday. Clear the ice out from around your dens before it melts. Then we will feast."

As the crowd dispersed, Mardor growled loudly, "This strange ice isss another warning to leave this strange land, while we still can."

Drakor kept walking, unwilling to confront his nemesis. He had enough problems to deal with already. But Mardor's smoldering eyes followed him, with enough fire to melt all the ice that had fallen.

Jardor tilted his head toward the giant. "Mardor isss like an angry Volcano."

Drakor nodded. "He hates me. His friends look forward to my defeat. Older dragons have more years of good memories on our island, before we were hungry, so this change isss harder for them. And they want a proper, older leader."

Jardor shook his head. "You are a better leader than they realize, better than you realize. You turned a weird green sky into a celebration. Then you made a freaky ice storm seem interesting, not scary."

Drakor smiled. "It isss a challenge to find the right words. I never had to think so hard, before I won."

Jardor laughed. "Yes, you did. You won with your mind, not your size."

Dragons busily filled buckets with ice and dumped them near the stream. Drakor scanned their ice-covered village as he dug. Why would their hot Volcano send ice? And how could a warm sky dump so much ice, so fast? He shook his head and kept digging.

The hailstones soon melted together into slick, pebbly ice. Youngsters gathered on the icy field to play Slam, hitting a flat skipping stone with their tails. But their play was more like a rough game of tag as they gleefully slammed into each other whenever they could.

Drakor asked the dams to take turns keeping an eye on the youngsters, to make sure they stayed close to the village. The dwire were probably watching.

* * *

Scree caught a glimpse of bright blue in the coral forest. This was a deadly blue-ringed octopus. It had the most potent poison in the sea!

She made several journeys across the sea, leading their fleet of skiffs, moving the pod to safety. As she left on the last trip, dangerous new volcanic gases bled into the sea. Finally, the small, blue-ringed octopi clambered aboard the pod skiffs. They squeezed into every crevice. Sharks and turtles swam right beside the small skiffs, ignoring each other, fleeing from the growling volcano.

She scanned their new reef. Hidden within this crystal forest, the blue-ringed octopi lived in their simple homes: a jumble of rocks, a coral cavity, or an empty shell. They had spread throughout Scree's village, making this a safer place for her pod.

Scree waved to her tiny, toxic neighbors. The blue-ringed octopus allies traded their powerful venom for Orm's blue-green abalone pearls, which Scree traded for dragon products. She smiled. Her unexpected friendship with one dragon had grown to include the entire clan of golden dragons.

Scree patted her precious Healer bag. This was made from indestructible cloth-of-gold, woven from the thin, wiry roots of pen shells. The bright fabric was covered with tiny, dull brown shells sewn on for camouflage. Four compartments held a treasure-trove of supplies, including this deadly venom and a sharp surgeon's knife of glittering black garnet. As a Healer, she often explored the border between life and death: knives and poison could heal or kill.

She squeezed her suckers, feeling the wax balls that were filled with venom. Poisonous pearls. She had challenged a horde of giant squid in the dark abyss, alone, to protect the pod. Arak helped her survive by creating these toxic balls. Now, every pod member carried a poison ball hidden in a sucker.

This poisonous protection was changing octopus culture more than anything else.

Naturally timid octopi were becoming fearless. Hiding in plain sight was their traditional defense, but now this camouflage was mainly used for hunting or games.

Scree flowed over to Orm's cave. She found her mate just outside, juggling three large pearls: pink, lilac, and black. She reached into her pouch and tossed him two more shimmering balls. "The pearl farms are doing well?"

Orm smoothly added her peach pearls to his juggling routine, braiding five paths through the sea. He spoke with two more arms, "All the farms are doing great. Soon we'll have enough pearls to trade." He caught each lustrous ball as it sank through the sea, adding them to his lumpy bag.

Scree applauded, turning her arms dragon-gold and adding scales to signal the highest praise.

Orm gave a proper bow, bending just below the

mantle. He gazed west, toward the distant shore, and his arms became stiff. "I'm not ready for a clan-and-pod gathering. Pearls move much faster in air, and I haven't practiced sky juggling for many moons."

Scree twined arms with her mate, feeling his worry. He was often chosen to share the First Octopus legend, with its traditional pearl dance. "Let's visit the raft. You can practice with pearls while I check on the skiffs."

Orm's stiff arms relaxed into normal curves. "That's an excellent idea."

Scree looked toward the distant farms. "Orm, will we have food to share?"

"With golden dragons?"

"And ice dragons. If Drakor has a restless, hungry clan of ice dragons, then the golden dragons will be in danger. Everything is connected."

Orm nodded. "Good point. The crops are growing well here, so we should have extra."

Scree pointed to a web of light dancing on the sand. The glowing pattern was made by waves at the surface, where the peaks caught the sun. This formed bright lines of condensed light that shone down through the water. "Sky and sea connect in interesting ways . . ."

Orm finished, "Like dragons and octopi." He copied the dancing light onto his skin. Then he replaced this light pattern with two simple, interlocking shapes: dragon and octopus. They fit together perfectly in an abstract, repeating design that covered his body. He played with the colors, turning a pattern of gold dragons with happy-green octopi into silvery-white dragons with challenge-blue octopi. The design colors flashed back and forth on his body.

41

Scree stared. "You're the ultimate artist! I can't wait for the next dragon-and-octopus festival. Feasting, story-telling, rainbow fires, and trade! We left so much behind."

Orm shook his head. "We saved what matters most: the entire pod and our blue-ringed octopus friends. We'll trade for what we need, especially spearheads and dragon spices."

Scree laughed. "We need spearheads, but I think spices are a *want*."

"No. Tasty meals are a *need*."

Stur, the pod leader, dropped down through the sea and landed neatly beside them. He twined arms respectfully with both pod members. "Orm, at the New Moon Festival, could you tell the story of our battle with the giant squid?"

Orm bowed. "I'll be ready."

A smile flitted across Scree's face as she studied her former fosterling. He had grown into a strong pod leader. "Stur, I spoke with Arak in trance-mind. Our volcano became an island, and it's still growing. It must have destroyed our village."

Stur nodded. "You were right, our volcano was the bigger problem, but we still had to survive the squid attack before we could move. When you visited the abyss, did you find any signs of the giant squid? And what have you learned about the fish?"

Scree flushed pink with surprise. How did he know? But Stur was clever. Maybe he could read this in the currents. If only she could use the currents to spy on giant squid. Her arms stiffened. The migrating fish were scarce. Was something happening to them as they rode the currents?

Scree looked south. "I found signs of giant squid. I don't know what's happening to the fish. They could be dying from volcano chemicals or a different problem but, if squid are hungry, they may hunt us again. The pod should plan a defense and practice throwing spears."

Stur nodded. "I agree. And I'd like you to lead this defense. Again."

Scree barely stopped a scream of angry red. Her arms tensed with worry and her main brain shouted, *NO! The mystery could be the greater danger!* She calmed her many minds.

Stur gave a half-smile as her arms relaxed.

Scree stretched taller. "I'll prepare the defense if I'm in charge of prisoners. I will not kill."

Stur bowed. "I know, and I accept your terms."

Scree held up an arm. "And I'll train Scrim to take my place. I can't just wait around here."

His arms stiffened. "We need *you*."

"Scrim will do just as well. We must understand the other mysteries."

Stur nodded, but he walked away on stiff, frustrated arms.

Scree sketched a diagram in the sand. "Orm, there aren't enough of the migrating fish here. They catch a ride on the currents to breed and feed. What if the adults and hatchlings aren't completing the circle to return home?"

She shuddered as a cold finger of the sea ran across her mantle, as if in warning.

* * *

Drakor flicked his tail as the sun rose, painting the sky with bright topaz and ruby streaks. Dawn always had the same fiery colors of Volcano flames. When would the

43

other sky colors return?

Morning mist rose like smoke from the stream. Drakor avoided the slick, mossy boulders as he jumped into the frigid water, claws out. He caught his breakfast and ate it raw. It was odd how much he missed the cooked, spiced meals from the short time he lived with the golden dragons.

Drakor walked back to the village, checking first on the new dragon-dam. She was building her nest between her den and a neighbor's den, safely in from the edge of the village. He nodded approval. On their island, nests were built near the hot springs, far from their village. But the New World had more dangers, so nesting within the village was the best choice.

Her elegant nest was built from fist-sized stones of dark granite, but there were only a few gemstones fitted into the crevices. Dragon nests usually had so many gems that they glowed like a fiery Volcano. There was a thick layer of dried red grass, which would cushion her egg. But this grass was a poor substitute for the glassy, golden-red Volcano threads used for nests in their old home. Drakor felt another jolt of mourning for their lost island.

The dragon-dam flicked her tail nervously as she bowed to Drakor. "Soon I will lay my egg, but there are no hot springs here. How should I warm my nest?"

Drakor clicked his claws together. How indeed? Their new Volcano was silent, with no life-giving warmth. On their island, generations of dragons had nested on the warm ground of the hot springs. Was this why Mardor objected to a new home without this? But if the clan had stayed on the island, they would all be dead.

"Ask Merika. She might have ideas." Drakor gave

the dam three small, brilliant gemstones: ruby, topaz, and sapphire. "I brought these from our old home. Use them for your nest, for tradition."

She bowed her thanks, but her tail flicked up and down with worry.

Drakor left, flicking his own tail uneasily. Maybe his second-in-command would have a solution.

Jardor shrugged his wings. "I know nothing about nesting, but we could make Volcano gems. Adding bright stones to her nest might cheer her up."

Drakor growled, "I think she isss more worried about the health of her egg than the look of her nest."

Jardor nodded. "Yes, but I do not know what else to do."

Drakor's wings stretched upward as he gazed into the west. "Neither do I, and today isss a good day to fly. We can search for dwire and sunset dragons." He leapt up into the wind, tasting the freedom of the sky, and escape.

They flew northwest, skimming just above the trees. Drakor scanned back and forth, searching for dwire or the legendary sunset dragons, but all he saw was the endless forest.

The sun was high overhead when Drakor reached the lonely cone. Trees had been swallowed up by Volcano blood that later cooled into stone. Rock trunks and stumps stood dark and silent in the ghostly remains of a dead forest. Saplings and scruffy bushes grew in the ashes.

Drakor inhaled the comforting smells of old ash mixed with scents of young growth. It felt like home, but this Volcano had returned to deep sleep. The ground did not tremble. There were no sharp, annoying sulfur smells, but also no warm springs to help a nesting dragon. Could a dragon's egg hatch in this New World? Any problems would be another reason to challenge him as leader.

Drakor stretched the worry out of his body. He channeled the sky, sending lightning swords into the volcanic ash below. Jardor threw his swords, too, in a friendly competition for the most strikes. Then they swooped down together to collect the newly made stones.

Each lightning strike melted the ground, fusing ash into a glassy, emerald green stone. Drakor grinned as he juggled five gems, tossing them high into the sky. Then he caught and stored them.

They flew to the other side of the volcano and threw more lightning swords. This ash melted into ruby-red or sapphire-blue stones.

Drakor hefted a glassy gem twice the size of a dragon's eye. Sunlight passed straight through, making a bright ruby stain on the pale ash. These were perfect gems of fire.

The dragons sat down on cold rock logs with their tails hanging down behind. Volcano blood had hardened around these fallen trees to create excellent dragon seats. They snacked on orange tubers and smoked fish from their chest pouches. Then Drakor spread his wings wide, soaking up the pale afternoon sun.

Jardor peered through an emerald-green gem. "These are of the Volcano, perfect for an ice dragon's nest."

Drakor nodded. "And, we have more than the dragon-dam needs. I hope we can use the rest of these gems for trade."

Jardor put the gems in his pouch. "What isss trade?"

"We would exchange stuff with the golden dragons, so we each get something we want."

Jardor shrugged his wings. "Maybe we could just work harder."

Drakor clicked his claws together. "More types of food would help us survive the long winter. If we could trade for chocolate, ice dragons would be more cheerful. But trade isss more than just a way to get something we want. Trading helps you become friends. Golden dragons and octopi trade with and help each other. Now both groups are stronger."

Jardor frowned. "How can an octopus help a dragon?"

Drakor laughed. "You have not met Scree, or Orm. I will tell you a story on our way home." He stretched his wings, and the slanting afternoon light produced a monstrous shadow-dragon. If only he could grow as fast as his shadow, into a huge dragon who looked like a proper leader.

CHAPTER 6: TRANCE-STONE

Morning fog drifted away as Drakor strode to the dragon's nest, juggling five Volcano stones. These looked just like their traditional nest gems, but real rubies, emeralds, and sapphires were hard to find here. He presented these gemstones to the dragon-dam.

She tucked the gems among the plain stones, giving her nest the proper look of a fiery Volcano. But she continued to flick her tail nervously.

Drakor shuddered as a shaft of light ran across her wing. The tips had turned a darker shade of silvery-white. Soon the dam would have an egg to warm, and he still had no idea how to help. How could he call himself a leader? His tail drooped to the ground as he trudged away.

Drakor caught a young dragon-lady studying him, with an odd gleam in her eyes. He quickly turned away. He was much too busy for a mate of his own! Some day he might give nest stones to a dragon-lady, but not for many years.

Drakor tucked the rest of his Volcano gems under a long slab of clear quartz. The gems sparkled up from below, like stones in a wild stream. This unique shelf held a few stone plates and mugs for the evening communal meal.

Drakor flew off to gather more of the branches that were torn off by the storm. He carried armloads to the smokehouse and stacked them in separate piles, since each type of wood made a different flavor of smoked fish. When winter dragged on, and all they had left was fish, any variety would be welcome. Satisfied, he left to join the dragons working on another storage pit.

A dank, earthy aroma rose from the deep hole. Drakor inhaled deeply and laughed. Why did he still miss the sharp, stinky odors of their old home? Dragons were often hungry, scrounging for food, yet he missed that harsh, beautiful island.

Scraping noises came from the pit. Then a rope at the surface jerked twice. Drakor hauled the bucket up, hand over hand, claws back to protect the rope. He emptied the rocky dirt into another bucket, and a dragon carried it away. Finally, Drakor called down the hole. "It isss deep enough. Climb up the claw-holds."

Jardor climbed out of the pit while Drakor pointed to two dragons. "Please pave the floor with those large, flat river stones." As they left, he motioned to a group of dragon-dams. "Please bring the tubers and smoked fish."

Jardor dusted his hands off and grinned. "We now have two storage pits!"

Drakor clouted his friend on the back. "Excellent. We just need a few more."

A dragon-lord growled, "More? Two isss more than enough."

Another grumbled, "He wants to keep us too busy to miss our true home."

Drakor flexed his claws with frustration but kept his voice calm. "Our Volcano erupted. The island isss gone. According to our legends, this winter will be longer, so we must store more food."

He turned back to Jardor. "Walk with me."

The sun was now low in the sky, adding the typical flames of sunset. Drakor stopped when they reached the edge of the village. "Jardor, I must leave. Could you manage the clan and keep us on schedule for digging?"

His second-in-command simply nodded. "How long will you be gone?"

Drakor cocked his head to the side. "You did not ask where."

Jardor grinned. "No. But why?"

"Much has changed. I need a quiet space to think."

Jardor met his eyes. "Isss it so hard to be leader?"

Drakor sighed. "I grow tired of the watching eyes. I am used to more freedom."

Jardor pointed to a cluster of branches floating on the lake. "You take the right sticks and I'll take the left. First dragon to strike five, wins."

They each channeled the sky, throwing lightning swords. Branches burst into flames and pine smoke drifted ashore.

Drakor was faster.

Jardor thumped his friend on the back. "You won this game, just like you always do. You are still the same dragon. Go and do what you need to do. The clan will still be here when you return."

Drakor nodded. "Mind-call if you need me." He flew due west until he was above the hills. Then he flew straight up through the thick clouds, wrapped in cold, gray mist. He turned north, hidden from prying eyes by the solid white carpet below. These clouds flowed across the sky like a river, parted around a lone mountain peak, and joined together again downstream.

Every landmark was hidden by the clouds, so he used an inner map. All dragons could close their eyes and see the magnetic field that flowed around the world. Drakor had trained his mind to watch within while his eyes were open, a skill needed for lightning sword games. He flew with open eyes while following the magnetic lines that glowed silvery-gray in his mind.

The sun set just as Drakor reached the ice cave, his secret retreat in the glacier. Moonlight glowed through the frozen walls and sparkled along cracks, like stars. This cave was a silent haven of glassy blues and whites, like a frozen sky. He breathed fire into a snow-filled hollow in the rock floor. Steam rose as he melted a pool of water and heated it to boiling.

Drakor took a sparkling mug from his pouch. With one claw, he lightly touched each of the gems that formed a rainbow circle around the clear crystal. The center diamond matched his clear quartz globe, his trance-stone. This blue-and-white ceramic mug was a precious gift from Arak's clan.

Drakor fixed a calming tea with dried mint and chamomile. He sipped slowly, relaxing into the memories of his time with the golden dragons. When a dragon learned to communicate in trance-mind, the clan celebrated with a tea ceremony. Soon, he would teach ice dragons to enter the trance-mind and mind-talk. With practice, they could share thoughts across long distances. Then he would add a new tradition: a special mug to celebrate set with a gem that matched their trance-stone.

It was time to call Arak. Drakor took the trance-stone from his pouch, calmed his mind, and focused into the clear quartz globe. He entered the trance-mind and mind-traveled south.

Arak. I must visit

When

I can be there in two more dawns. Can we meet at that field north of the cave

Yes. Why there

I wish I had time to visit with the clan, but I must return quickly

Drakor's trance-mind returned to his limp body. He stored the precious globe, stretched out on a thick bed of leaves, and dropped into a deep, trouble-free sleep.

* * *

The light of a nearly full moon washed through the sea. Scree felt the changing symphony of the sea, as reef residents prepared for the high tide. She carried another meal to Strike, who stood guard over a mass of pinkish-orange eggs, flexing his tail to move water across them.

The mantis clicked his thanks. Then he spoke with gestures and light. "Scree, why did you help me? The first time?"

Scree focused on the light. Each color had a different meaning, and so did the flashing patterns. Her main brain *must* have grown from trying so hard to count the rapid light flashes!

She sketched a triangle in the sand. "You drew this sign."

His eyestalks twitched. "I saw you make that shape once, using your arms. What does it mean?"

Scree shook with silent laughter. "You didn't even know? That's the Healer sign. The triangle has a broad base of knowledge and the tipping point where healing happens. When you drew that sign, you called out the Healer in me."

Strike shimmered with new patterns. He must be laughing with light.

The next evening, a full moon rose above the sea. Silvery light filtered down through coral branches, making watery shadows across the reef. Scree turned a cheerful green. The mantis eggs were hatching! She held perfectly still as tiny orange larvae kicked out of their shells.

An hour later, the last hatchling floated up toward the surface to ride the currents.

Strike hung his head.

Scree signed, "What's wrong? Almost all of your eggs hatched."

He stared into the distance. "I mated for life. My mate is dead, so these were my last hatchlings. There's no one to share my burrow."

She nodded. "Strike, you would be a remarkable Healer. You see light I can only imagine. I feel/taste sickness, but you could actually *see* the sick cells inside a patient. With your help, I could target a micro-zap to the exact spot. You could make a burrow under my cave and help in my clinic."

Strike shook his jewel-colored head. "No. I'm a fighter."

Scree stood taller. "Then fight for others." Her arms jerked as border chimes sounded an alarm through the sea, and her body. She flushed gray with worry. It took something big to trigger those alarms! Scree checked the currents, tasting no new deaths in the sea. Her arms relaxed, and she pulsed to the center of their village.

Stur, the pod leader, turned gold to catch everyone's attention. "Travel in your groups of four to your assigned area. Search the border and stay camouflaged."

Three hours later, Stur called off the search.

Scree stared south, toward the abyss. "Orm, we still don't know what triggered that alarm. A harmless whale shark? Or a hungry giant squid?"

Orm grimaced. "A scout planning another attack?"

Scree sighed. "When will the warning system be finished?" She helped the pod plant kelp all around their village. As the seaweed trees grew taller, the octopi attached another set of shells or metal rods. These sets clanked together to sound an alarm.

Each alarm made a unique vibration, to quickly identify the place where the warning was triggered. This would help the pod prepare a swift, strong defense.

Orm pointed up. "The kelp trees are growing fast. They've nearly reached the surface!"

Scree made skin pictures of leafy kelp that raced up her body. "Good. The giants are interesting friends, but we'll need this warning if any challenge us. At least we

54

understand this squid danger. I'm more concerned with what we don't understand. What does this odd feel/taste mean? And what's happening with the fish? Are they dying here, or leaving and dying somewhere else?"

Scree waved a greeting to Krees and Tor, her former fosterlings. The youngsters turned happy-green and waved back. How had they grown so much? They were nearly her size! Where did the time go?

Scree pulsed back home, changing colors with her memories. She chose her fosterlings from the tiny new juveniles that arrived. She trained them in the ways of the pod and to be Healers. Scrim, another fosterling, was preparing to lead the defense against an attack. Just in case.

She stiffened at an unexpected, sharp clicking.

Strike poked his head out from beneath her cave. "I decided to make a new burrow here."

Scree signed, "How do you like it?"

Strike flashed a light pattern. "Adequate. Some may think I have an octopus guard but, truly, you now have a mantis guard." Then he shimmered with patterns she could barely see. The light faded away as it moved beyond her range of sight.

Scree smiled. Once again, Strike was laughing with light.

* * *

Drakor opened his eyes and stared. Golden sunrise glowed through the ice walls, as if the entire cave was carved from flame quartz! He ate a quick breakfast and launched into the sky, heading south, flying ever higher until he found the wind-stream. This current was bitterly cold, but much faster.

His nerves were frayed from dragon-weeks of dealing with the clan, and especially Mardor. He relaxed into a rhythmic flight, letting the solitude renew him.

Drakor landed on the pebble beach at sunset. Sky colors played across the waves in shades of fire, like gemstones: topaz, carnelian, ruby. Then stars shone in the darkness. He lay on the pebbles, away from the forest, soothed by the rhythmic surf. He slept well, knowing that the stones would squeak a warning if anything large approached, like dwire.

Drakor awoke before dawn. He soared high as the rising sun glowed up through the clouds below. Cherry red fire filled the spaces between purple-gray puffs, as if the world was burning. The clouds caught fire, glowing bright orange, then turning gold. He gazed at the color-changing carpet. This was the magic of flying.

As he drew near the field, Drakor felt a strong magnetic pull. His inner eye saw a bright, silvery-gray spot. Arak must have brought the lodestones! He dropped below the clouds, searching, and caught a glint of gold.

Drakor arrowed down, back-winged, and landed. "Arak! It isss so good to see you!"

The golden dragon grinned and held up a steaming mug. "You must be half-frozen."

Drakor's eyes glowed as he reached down for the mug. "Thanks. It isss cold in the wind-stream." He took a long drink. "Spiced red root tea! I have missed this." He finished the tea and sighed. "Dragon spices. Cinnamon, nutmeg, ginger, honey, a pinch of pepper, and Dorali's special herbs." He bowed low to his friend. "Thank you. For everything."

Arak shrugged his wings. "You had the hardest part,

fighting Mardor. Dorali made this tea special for you. She wants to know how your wing held up on the long flight here." He eyed the white dragon up and down, then nodded. "You look well. You've grown! And you made good time flying here."

Drakor grinned, displaying his long, sharp teeth. "I am well, I needed to grow, and I am learning the sky currents of our new home. This place has layers of wind that move in different directions." He cocked his head to one side. "I did not think you would move here so soon."

Arak sighed. "Two great waves struck our home. They tore down our trees, stole the beach, and scoured the ocean floor. Coral chunks that weighed more than Mardor fell on the shore. Even worse, the waves covered our cave. Saltwater flowed in through hidden holes and ruined part of our stored food. Then the storm struck, taking the rest of the tree flowers. There won't be a fall harvest."

Arak flexed his wings distractedly. "Thick rafts of floating gray stones washed up along the shore. Dragonlets bounced across this wiggly playground-on-the-sea, laughing. But I felt as gray as the stones. This raft was made from the bones of your home, and that eruption sent tsunamis that clawed ours down, too. The gray snowfall of ash made it hard to breathe. So, we had few reasons to stay."

Drakor solemnly bowed his head. "My home was doomed to die, but I hoped yours would be spared." He looked to the east. "Even here, far from our old home, dead fish and strange skeletons are washing up on the shore. Scree isss right, everything isss connected."

Arak stretched his wings wide and folded them straighter, as if shaking off the loss. "The copper was safe, and part of our food survived the waves. Taron and I are taking turns making the long trips, moving dragons and supplies to the New World. Sometimes I wish we could all just fly here, like ice dragons, but it's too far."

Drakor shivered. "That was a difficult flight, even for us. It was brutally long, bitterly cold, and we lost a dragon. How are your ice dragon guests?"

Arak bowed his head. "I'm sorry for the loss. But, any dragon who stayed would have died. Our guests are doing well. The dragon-dam is nervous, her dragonlet is loved by all, and your sire is an amazing storyteller! We'll be sad to see him leave."

Drakor whipped around and dropped to a fighting crouch as a branch bent and sprang back. There was only sound, with nothing to see. He turned back to Arak, and his wings slowly relaxed. "I thought that was a dwire, but the branch did not bend enough, and the sounds were too small."

Arak's eyes grew wide. "You're ready for a fight! Those are just tree lizards. They camouflage, too. They're useful in our new cave, eating bugs that would eat our stored food. Have you met the dwire?"

"Not yet, but they are near our village. I wish we could *see* them."

Arak nodded. "That would be useful. You've flown a long way to visit. How can we help?"

Drakor stood taller, automatically assuming a leaderly stance. "According to legend, winter isss long and harsh after a Volcano explodes. We brought little food with us on our long flight here. Our lake has fish, and we gathered old nuts, but that storm has destroyed much of our future harvest. We need more plant foods.

Would your clan be able to trade?"

Arak nodded slowly. "This will be a harsh winter for all of us, but we'll trade what we can when we bring the ice dragons home. Scree might be able to help, too. You have your claws full. I don't want dragons to have an excuse to challenge your rule."

Drakor growled, "Mardor will need no excuse. He will make one."

Arak nodded again. "Be careful. What would you trade?"

"The lake fish are huge! Their skins are perfect for skiff-wings, and we have smoked fish." Drakor took three bright stones from his pouch: red, blue, and green. Each was larger than his eye. "We make gems from Volcano ashes."

Arak hefted the clear stones and used his metal knife in a scratch test. "These look just like ruby, sapphire, and emerald. They test softer, so they'd be easier to carve." He put them in his chest pouch. "We can always use more fish and fish-skins. I'll see what food we can spare."

Arak stretched his wings. "We've mostly been fixing up our new cave, but a group of dragons flew south and harvested sacks of cocoa pods. Those odd trees are inland, surrounded by hills, so they escaped the worst of the storm damage. It seems that their fruit grows all year long! Zarina should be able to make extra chocolate to trade."

Drakor snapped his tail. "That would be great!"

Arak took a small bag from his pouch. "This is Dorali's special tea, to drink if you must fight. She's working with Orm to make something even better."

Drakor placed the bag carefully into his chest pouch.

"Thank them for me. I may need this."

Then Arak handed him a clear quartz jar with bluish-green powder and a cork stopper. "These are the copper salts you asked for. It's great, being so close to our copper mine! If you need more, we have plenty to spare. Why do you want it?"

Drakor gave him a mysterious smile. "Thank you. When you visit, you will see."

Arak lifted up a lumpy sack. "I thought you'd miss these."

Drakor hugged the sack close, as if it held a precious dragon egg. The sack was heavier than it looked, and his inner eye nearly screamed at the blinding-bright silvery-gray. "Our lodestones! Thank you for bringing them. Our flight here was long, and extra weight meant death." These stones were an important part of ice dragon heritage, used for their Winter games. After losing so much, they meant even more. He carefully secured the sack inside his backpack.

Arak grinned. "I thought you might like to have some now. I'll bring the rest when we return the guests." He tugged a sack out from beneath a bush. "Here's food from Zarina to fuel your flight back." He eyed Drakor's broad chest. "You've grown more than I expected. I'm glad I listened to my mate and added more food."

Drakor took a deep breath, inhaling the aromas. His eyes held a dreamy expression. "Cinnamon-honey roasted almonds and smoked fish with pepper! I have missed your spices. Give Zarina my thanks. I wish I could stay and visit, but the clan isss restless."

Arak handed him one last bag. "This weighs little and will help calm your clan."

Drakor filled his lungs with the irresistible scent. "Chocolate!" He bowed low. "Thank you. Chocolate isss precious, but friendship isss the most precious gift."

Drakor launched into the sky, climbing fast. Far below, Arak zigged his claws in a jagged lightning path, wishing him a safe journey home.

The world below disappeared as Drakor flew up beyond the clouds. He could fly forever, far beyond his troubles, if he was not the leader. But no leader quit; he was beaten and replaced. And how could he stop being leader without risking his friends? Drakor stretched his wings and settled into an easy rhythm. He needed a plan.

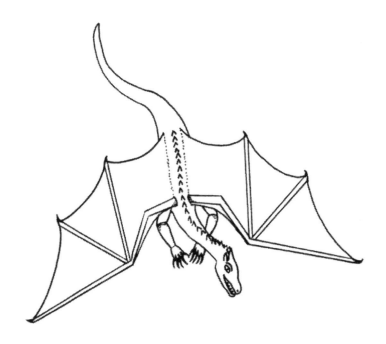

CHAPTER 7: DRAGON CLAWS

Drakor shivered as he stared to the west. Thick, ferocious clouds poured over the hills like an unstoppable tide, drowning each peak. Then the leading edge curled over like dragon claws and captured the last hill. Their village would be next.

Jardor snapped his tail. "I never saw such clouds! It looks like an avalanche of snow."

Drakor nodded. "This isss an interesting world. Spring isss too cold and the clouds act like dragons. I never know what to expect, so we need to be ready. You are my second-in-command. I want a third and fourth in-command."

"Why?"

Drakor clicked his claws together. "It isss hard to explain. I beat Mardor. One dragon. Now I can tell every dragon what to do. Isss that fair?"

Jardor grinned. "Mardor isss no normal dragon. What are you thinking?"

Drakor laughed. "True, Mardor isss not an average dragon. I was thinking about the golden dragons. They do not fight to become leader. They choose the leader that most of them think will do the best job. Then they share ideas and talk about problems. I want more in-commands to help and to share ideas. It isss a start."

Jardor nodded slowly. "Fighting isss our way, but there could be a better way. It isss something to think about. Cranart could make a good third-in-command. He isss older and good with lightning swords, but he does not seem to mind that you win those games. For the fourth, you could choose an older dragon-dam. They may have different ideas."

Drakor clouted him on the back. "You are the best second-in-command ever!"

Jardor turned and looked him in the eye. "You also need spies."

"Spies?"

"Mardor used spies when he was leader. He still does. You need all the help you can get."

Drakor sighed. "True. But I do not want to become Mardor."

Jardor laughed. "That isss not possible. He isss the biggest dragon ever!"

Drakor flexed his claws. "Mardor isss training to fight. I think he will challenge me."

Jardor snapped his tail. "That isss against the rules.

You beat him."

"I think the rules have changed. We have a new home, new leader, and new ways. Everything changed too fast. The older dragons are upset. They want something that feels safe, strong, and familiar. That isss Mardor. I have seen him talking to these dragons, and they stop talking when I get close. He isss trying to turn the clan against me."

Drakor gazed into the distance, flicking his tail up and down. "Mardor was the clan leader my whole life. I wanted *him* to lead the clan to safety. Instead, I became the leader. I do not know if I can win another fight."

Jardor rustled his wings nervously. "What will you do?"

Drakor gave a lopsided smile. "I will try. I am practicing to fight, in secret. And I have something better than spies: friends. Now I need to call a meeting."

They flew to the circle, and Drakor landed in the center. Jardor struck the huge drum once. The beat rumbled through the morning sky, summoning the dragons. Soon the rings were full.

Drakor raised his wings high. The dragons gradually grew quiet, while Mardor grinned at the slow response. Drakor's hands automatically curled into fists. He forced them open. "The golden dragons will bring our clan members home soon. Then we will trade our Volcano gems and fish for their food and chocolate.

Wings fluttered and dragons whispered, "*Chocolate.*"

A young dragon-lord raised his wing. "What isss trade?"

"Ice dragons and golden dragons will agree on how much we will give each other for one big fish, or a clawfull of gems, or chocolate."

A dragon-lady raised a wing, and he nodded to her. "I can carve gemstone bowls to trade for chocolate."

Mardor raised a wing part way up and growled, "Why should we trade? We are much bigger. We can easily *take* what we want."

Drakor stared him down. "They are *dragons*. They would fight back, and even ice dragons can be hurt." He glanced to the south. "Attacking the golden dragons would be like cutting down the tree to get all the nuts. The tree would make no more nuts. Golden dragons would spend their time fighting, not gathering food or making chocolate. Then there isss nothing to gain."

Drakor looked from one dragon to the next, meeting their eyes. "Trade isss better than fighting. We catch many fish and make gems from worthless ashes. We can trade to get food and chocolate from golden dragons. With trade, there isss no loss."

A dragon-lord asked, "When will we trade?"

"The golden dragons will arrive in a moon to bring the ice dragons home. Then we will trade."

Mardor raised his wing and began speaking without permission. "Why do yellow dragons help ice dragons? Do they need us to get fish for them? Fish too big for them to catch?"

Drakor's hands began to clench in anger. He took a deep, calming breath and uncurled them. "Golden dragons are smaller, but they are also clever and strong. Size isss *not* everything. They do *not* need our help. They carried our newest dragonlet away from the Volcano, so she could be safe from the explosion. They want us to survive because we are all dragons."

Mardor sneered, "You say our home isss gone, that we survive because of you. But nobody has seen our home to know if it isss really gone. Isss this just a sun dream?"

Dragons looked from Drakor to Mardor, flicking their tails nervously.

Drakor stretched taller, puffed out his chest, and held his wings in crisp folds, trying to look like the leader they wanted. Like Mardor. "You heard the explosion from across the sea, when our Volcano left to join the stars. You feel/see the change in the magnetic field. You felt the power of that storm. Sunsets are brighter than ever, like fire. Our island isss gone. One day we may be able to see the empty place that was our home. But we have a new home *here*. Do you remember how hungry we were? Now we catch fish every day."

Drakor looked to the east, toward the sea. "An ocean giant once said that home isss where you are. Wherever we go, we have the freedom of the sky. Here we have food, too."

A few tails flicked up and down, up and down. The rhythm was catching. Young dragons and some older ones began snapping their tails up and down like a wind-blown field. A group of dragon-dams joined in, adding to this signal of approval.

Drakor scanned the crowd and smiled. "I need volunteers to make items for us to trade."

Wings rose around the circles.

He assigned dragons to make Volcano gems and to carve bowls. Then he ended the meeting, while Mardor glared at him through slitted eyes. Drakor turned away from the giant, relaxing his tense muscles knot after knot.

He desperately needed solitude, but found his feet walking toward Merika's den. He caught up with his friend partway to her home.

She turned and gave him a warm smile. "Come see the new plants!" They walked together to her den.

Merika pointed to a planter just inside the entrance, where small green shoots breached the soil. Her eyes glowed. "The ice-flower plant just sprouted! When this long winter ends, I can plant young bushes near the forest. In a few seasons, we can make our traditional drink with the berries to properly celebrate the Summer Solstice."

Drakor stared at the tiny plants. This was a piece of home, a memory made real. These were true ice dragon plants, with snow-white flower petals that turned as clear as ice when it rained. The small berries were blue, the color of the sky, of freedom. "That isss great news! I did not know you brought seeds."

Merika watered the plants carefully. She pointed. The edge of her den was lined with rough stone planters, all with seedlings, with different shapes and shades of green. "I brought many types of seeds. That isss the treasure I chose from our home."

Drakor smiled. "You are wise."

Merika looked to the east. "Our island home isss truly gone?"

Drakor nodded. "Yes."

Merika squared her wings. "Then we will make a better home here. Thank you again for the strike-stones." She placed a copper pot over the small stone pit and lit a fire with sparks from the golden stones. When the water boiled, she made two mugs of herbal tea. Spicy steam filled the den. "I think you need this. That was a difficult meeting."

They drank together in a comfortable silence.

Drakor relaxed on the stone bench, surrounded by the reassuring scents of homeland plants. But after he left, his thoughts returned to Mardor, and his hands became fists. This was not over. Soon, Mardor or another dragon would challenge him to be leader. And then . . . Worries grew in his mind like the shadows that thickened around him.

* * *

Scree sampled the sea with her arms, feeling the delightful flavors. "Spices! And chocolate!"

Orm grinned. "It's the New Moon Festival."

Three strong beats on a giant clam shell announced the feast.

Scree turned happy-green as these vibrations washed through her body. "It's our first proper celebration in the New World." She jetted to the feasting table with Orm and joined the line, where octopi flashed cheerful colors.

Scree eyed the unfinished table. This was a rough jumble of round, dead coral rocks. In time, there would be hundreds of rocks carefully fitted together, making an elegant table to keep the feast above the sandy grit. But the food was already perfect.

Orm pointed. "Desert!"

Bright orange scallops were clustered together at the far end of the table. These hinged shell pairs held precious balls of chocolate that were coated with nut oils, to protect them from the sea.

Scree laughed. "First, the main dishes." She made a ring of scallops around the edge of her coral plate, filling the middle with a colorful seaweed salad. Then she arranged crab claws into a fancy star with eight points.

Orm glanced at her plate. "That's a flavorful star."

Scree grinned. "Your jellyfish design is exquisite. How did you get that glow? It's a nice touch."

He held up a crystal jar that glowed blue. "I made a tasty fungus sauce."

She turned both eyes to the glowing jar. "I love cold fire."

Scree filled her mug with red-root tea, pushed the top on, and settled onto the sand with friends. She studied the plate that Scrim held. Her apprentice had drawn a realistic squid with seaweed and small brown cockle shells. "That's a perfect design."

Scree watched her friend discreetly. Three of his arms had been torn off by a giant squid in their recent battle. Two of his missing arms had begun to regenerate, but the third had been ripped off into the mantle and would never re-grow.

Scrim would always have an awkward gap, so he might never move as fast as other octopi. But he was a deep thinker, clever and creative. And of all her apprentices, he was the one best suited to take her place as leader of the pod defense.

Scree savored the flavors of her edible art while pod-mates discussed their new homes and the best places to hunt. No one mentioned the recent seaquake, or giant squid, or the missing fish.

Scree signed to Orm, "They talk as if we left all our problems behind with this move. If only that were true."

A drummer began beating the giant clam shells. Dragon chimes joined the drumming, played with metal bars that hung free in the water. The music rippled pleasantly through Scree's body, adding a unique feel/sound to the natural symphony of the sea.

Scree's arms danced in the water, matching the irresistible beat that pulsed through the sea. Octopi moved onto the sandy dance floor, twirling and spinning with reckless abandon. Then Orm pulled her onto the dance floor, and she spun up into the sea.

Past and future fell away, lost in the whirling dance. Scree flashed a rainbow of understanding. Her pod-mates had just survived a battle, a move, and a seaquake. Now they were simply living in the moment, glad to be alive.

Beside the dance floor, youngsters played a game of Mimic. The leader changed her shape and colors to become a rare blue lobster. The players copied this in a heartbeat. Suddenly, eight blue lobsters sat on the sand.

A new beat rang through the sea, and everyone headed for the storyteller circle. This was well lit by glowfish. These fish were living lights, attracted to bowls with shredded clams.

Stur, the pod leader, moved to the center of the circle, and every arm fell silent. Pictures appeared on his mantle while two arms wove words through the water. "This is the legend of the First Octopus. Long ago, our mother, the Moon, ruled the seas. But she was lonely. So she gathered rich mud from the bottom of the sea and made a head. Then she added two arms for each of the four moon phases . . ."

When he finished, Scree joined the applause. She changed her arm color to bright dragon-gold with emerald spirals. Octopi changed their colors to every rainbow shade. The story circle became a fantasy garden of colorful octopus arms.

Next, Orm pulsed to the center. Octopi lowered their

speaking arms respectfully and sat in stillness. All eyes were focused on the master storyteller.

"This is the story of our battle with three giant squid." He spoke with eloquent gestures while a movie played across his body-screen. He made the fight vivid, terrifying, and real. When the last remaining squid smashed its monstrous arm down on Scree, everyone jumped.

Scree could still feel that tremendous blow, but she had survived. Others were less fortunate.

Orm finished the story and bowed.

The crowd went wild, waving golden arms with dragon scales. This was the highest praise.

Then Scrim told the story of their courageous move across the sea. He shared images of the fearsome storm waves in the last crossing, and cheerful green octopi pulsing down to their new home.

Again, the audience applauded. Scree made bright lightning twirl up her storm-colored arms. The fierce battle and daring move were *their* stories, and they would all be part of these legends.

Scree caught the leader's eye and nodded. He had chosen stories to remind the pod of the dangers *and* their inner courage.

She looked to the west. The golden dragons would soon complete their move to the New World. Then they'd celebrate with a clan-and-pod festival at the shore, trading goods and sharing legends. Story-tellers used gestures from dragons and octopi. When a dragon changed his mind, he spoke of changing his colors, like an octopus. And to show acceptance of change, an octopus stretched out two arms like the open wings of a dragon.

71

Scree twirled her arms restlessly. Drakor was having a hard time as leader. Would the difficult dragons stretch their wings wider and accept the changes? Or would a dragon challenge him? Could Drakor win another fight?

CHAPTER 8: LIGHTNING ROD

Drakor took a deep breath, savoring the rain-washed air. After the shower, the cloudless sky was a deeper blue. Red and yellow mushrooms had popped up all over the meadow. It was so rainy that these were the new flowers!

Drakor followed his nose to the smokehouse, where dragons were busy filleting five huge fish. "Good work." He flew to the village and landed near a cluster of young dragon-lords. They bowed and then stretched their wings wide, a sign borrowed from Arak.

Drakor smiled. Open wings were the new symbol for accepting ideas, change, and his leadership. He felt their eyes follow him as he continued walking.

Drakor walked by a cluster of old dragon-lords talking with Mardor. They fell silent and narrowed their eyes before barely nodding their heads. Mardor's eyes showed pure hatred. Drakor stretched taller and held his gaze until the former leader lowered his eyes.

Drakor turned away, feeling the angry eyes that burned into his back. He flicked his tail. For years, nobody noticed him. Now, eyes followed him everywhere. He was a lightning rod for eyes.

More disconcerting were the interested eyes of unmated dragon-ladies. They arched their necks and preened when he looked their way. But not his good friend Merika. Drakor shook his head. He was an upstart young leader in a new land trying to cope with angry dragons. He had no time for a mate!

Drakor turned at the quiet footsteps and smiled. Merika. She was so wonderfully predictable, a dragon he could depend on.

Merika handed him a large, steaming mug. "You need this."

"Thanks." He took a sip and smiled. "It isss tasty, but different. What did you use?"

"Chamomile to relax, berries for flavor and sweetness. Your wings are stiff, so your muscles must be tense."

Drakor gazed into her eyes. Calm eyes, a lovely, smoky gray. "How did you learn this?"

Merika flicked her tail. "Dorali taught me, when the golden dragons visited our island." She pointed to his chest pouch. "I have often wondered, what are those odd lumps?"

Drakor opened his pouch, releasing the aromas of

smoked fish and pine nuts. His shiny, silver water flask reflected the blue sky. Small quartz vials held metal powders.

Merika pointed to his large, silver-gray rock. "That isss a nice Titanium crystal! You have food, water, and ground metals: titanium for black lightning, cobalt for blue. We all carry this, but what isss in that lump?"

Drakor unwrapped a clear, fist-sized, eight-sided crystal.

Merika's eyes grew wide. "That diamond isss huge! And it must be heavy. Why do you always carry it?"

Drakor stared into the sparkling depths, remembering the scent of his dam. She had a pleasant, piney smell from the pine needles that she heaped onto his small sleeping pallet. She hummed a dragon's lullaby, but he always stayed awake to hear the whole tune. Instead, he fell asleep to her rhythmic breathing.

This crystal seemed to hold her spirit, like the diamond that brought the First Dragon to life. "My dam gave this to me before she died, when I was barely from the shell. This isss all I have from her. I wish I could have known her longer, before she left to join the stars."

Merika put gentle claws on his arm. "I am sorry she left so soon."

Drakor shrugged his wings in the ice dragon way. "It isss life." He tilted his head back, noted the growing clouds, and added, "I watch the stars at night to see her."

Merika met his eyes. "She watches you and isss proud." They stood silently, side by side, gazing into the sky. Then she asked, "What do you keep in the bottom?"

Drakor reached into a deep inner pocket. He pulled out a clear quartz ball and then his carved wood flute.

Last was a ceramic mug, made from blue and white clay. There was a circle of rainbow gemstones on one side, surrounding a clear diamond. "These are gifts from golden dragons."

Merika snapped her tail. "These are well made." She reached a claw toward the mug. "That isss beautiful."

"Zarina made this for me when I first visited the land of the golden dragons. They welcomed me, healed my shattered wing, and asked for nothing in return."

Merika turned her head to the south. "Golden dragons see the world through different eyes. I will leave with them when their skiff brings our ice dragons home. I want to be a Healer. Think what I could have done for your sire when he was injured, so much more than just sharing my food with him."

Drakor's heart skipped a beat. Leave? Merika was the steady part of his life, a quiet listener, the calm center in his stormy world. "Merika, the food you shared was scarce and precious. Few were willing to help. You are helpful *here*. Why must you leave?"

She sighed. "Dorali helped fix your wing when it was shattered. I need to know this magic, and more. I will train with Dorali and any other Healers who will let me."

Drakor took a step back. She was serious. Merika was leaving?

She held her hands out, claws back, and he met them as he always had. Their hands fitted together perfectly. "Drakor, we have been friends since the egg. I will always be your friend. I need to be a Healer. This isss my chance."

Drakor took a deep breath, inhaling the odd scents from this unnatural weather. He slowly stretched his wings, trying to work out the painful stiffness. His whirling mind was another problem. "I think I need another mug of that calming tea. Could we walk?"

They headed for the meadow, followed by watching eyes. Wet grasses squelched beneath their feet. Drakor noted with interest that his stride automatically changed to match hers. Everything matched. Something clicked in his mind. "When will you return?"

"When I know enough to truly help. I will visit when I can." Merika searched his eyes. "I see the looks that unmated dragon-ladies give to you, the leader. Their scales shine like never before. Many are strong and lovely. Soon you will choose one of them for a mate."

Drakor shook his head. "No. They only want me because I am the leader. That isss not what *I* want. Have you chosen another dragon?"

The buzzing of insects filled a silence that stretched longer and longer. Finally, Merika shook her head and whispered, "No."

Drakor smiled for the first time. "Then I will wait."

*　*　*

Scree flowed into Orm's cave and froze. Her eyes tracked a jellyfish that pulsed bright in the darkness. Its ice-clear body shone with inner light, like a captive aurora, glowing in rose and teal. Light gleamed along the tentacles.

In the blink of an eye, Scree became a shimmering, pink-and-blue jellyfish. She hung in the water while her tentacle-arms swayed with the gentle current.

Orm nodded approval. "You used your cell mirrors to catch the light. You almost glow!"

Scree changed back to her octopus shape, spiraled

down, and draped her arms comfortably over a rock seat. The water held a delicious feel/taste of fresh scallops with crushed mint leaves and garlic. This sea-and-land combination made the best meal!

One wall was covered with a living tapestry, an elegant design that glowed through the water in seven vibrant colors. She remembered when Orm first bred the small, clear, jelly-like tunicates to glow in colors. He created patterns by holding the base of each creature against the wall until it attached. Now he also bred glowing anemones. These animal-flowers added texture to his artwork.

Orm held an anemone against his skin. As soon as it attached, he added another glowing ornament. "Our sea flowers bloom all year long, so they're better than land flowers."

Scree nodded. "Anemones make the best gardens, colorful by day and glowing at night." She held an anemone against her skin, and the sea flower fastened on tight. Then she added another. Soon, her mantle had a necklace of anemones that glowed in red, orange, or blue.

Scree flexed her body, and the anemones stayed on. She dropped a pinch of crab meat into the center of each sea flower. "This should keep them in place, since only a hungry flower wanders off. These are perfect night lights."

Scree pulsed to the edge of the cliff with Orm. "Are you ready to explore? Remember, life speaks with light in the dark abyss."

Orm nodded. They each grabbed a rock and plummeted down into a dark, cold world.

Red colors vanished first, then orange and yellow,

like a melting rainbow. Soon, only blue, violet, and light beyond sight reached this eerie twilight world. A small octopus squirted luminous ink as it fled. Then a school of fish swept past with bright blue belly lights.

Scree held still, sorting the symphony that pulsed through her body. "Sound travels even faster in the abyss, so this is an efficient survey. The crabs and shrimp sound like they're doing well here. I feel the songs of young fish, but fewer adults and hatchlings. The missing notes are from some of the migrating fish."

Orm nodded. "And none of the chemicals that I taste should be killing fish."

Scree pointed down. "Let's check deeper." She dropped through darkness until she touched down on thick, squishy mud. Bristle worms and starfish of all kinds crawled across the vast mud floor. Her living lights showed only a few rocks, and these rare, solid anchors were completely covered with life.

Scree felt the rotting flavors of food that drifted down from far above. A feather star waved its frilly arms, grasping at this slow snowfall of death.

Orm held an arm out to feel/taste the stinky snow. He shook it off. "I'm glad we have better food. Scree, I sense nothing new here. Let's head back."

She formed a circle with two arms and then ripped the tips apart. "If the fish aren't dying here, they must be leaving and not returning. Where is the circle broken? We need to follow the currents to understand this problem. Everything is connected, so everyone could be hurt. Even the dragons."

Orm twirled his arms, not answering. Finally, he signed, "I assume you wish to follow in a skiff?"

Scree smiled. "Of course."

A three-foot fish with glowing green spots swam out of the murky distance.

Scree pointed. "Look! A *glowing* shark!"

Orm's eyes were huge. "That's a beautiful neon glow. But it's still a shark, and there's nowhere to hide."

Scree twined arms with her mate. "A skiff journey would be safer."

Orm made skiffs appear on his skin and then drenched them in towering waves. "Except for the storms."

Scree nodded. "But, thanks to our dragon friends, we now have proper skiff fins to surf the storms."

* * *

Drakor stood at the top of the hill, filling his lungs, tasting the cool wind after a shower. His claws clicked on the bare expanse of rock. This had a comfortable feel of home; it was once Volcano blood. The black rock held pieces of bright blue sky reflected in water-filled hollows. This matched the turquoise lake of their lost island.

Drakor shivered at the memory, and his eyes were drawn to the east like iron to a lodestone. The loss of their home was a raw wound for the ice dragons, and he alone *knew* that it was gone. Many still doubted their need to leave, to move to this strange land.

Something glittered in the scruffy bush, drawing him closer. Drops of morning dew clung to an invisible web, catching the light and sending it back even brighter. These sparkling strands triggered a memory. Arak had challenged him to make a plan to defeat Mardor and leave their doomed island. *The spider weaves a sticky trap for insects and makes safe strands to escape. It has a plan to survive. You need a plan.*

Drakor sighed. He fought Mardor to move their clan to safety. That solved one problem. Now he was the leader, trapped in a new web of problems. He blew gently on the web, and the spider scampered to safety, avoiding the dangerous strands. What plan could possibly avoid all the sticky new problems he faced? They seemed to grow faster than evening shadows. And what should he do about Mardor?

Jardor landed beside him and folded his wings neatly. "This isss your new favorite place."

Drakor turned his gaze to their village, which was a long glide away. "It isss quiet here."

Jardor raised one eye ridge. "There are decisions you must make as leader. Let me know how I can help." He followed Drakor's gaze to the cluster of older dragons. "I know why Mardor isss angry, but what about the others?"

Drakor sighed. "We had to leave before our home was destroyed. I had to lead the dragons here, quickly, while they were still too shocked to question the word of their new leader."

He looked Jardor in the eye. "I forced them to leave. But they never saw our island explode, so they do not see me as the dragon who saved their lives. I am the dragon who took them away from a home they knew and a leader they understood."

Jardor nodded. "Maybe it would help if these dragons could see that our old home isss gone."

"Perhaps. They forget how hungry we were on our island, but complain of every problem here. Then they blame me, the leader with all the power. But I do not control the weather or the world. It isss only an illusion of power."

Jardor cocked his head to the side. "You think a lot more. We used to play games and explore. We had fun."

Drakor shrugged his wings and winced. "Part of me wants to give up being leader. It isss hard to stand tall with my wings folded stiff, all the time, to look like the leader they expect. How did Mardor stand it?"

Jardor laughed. "He *wanted* to be leader."

Drakor sighed. "He *still* wants it. And we still need to solve the problem of the dwire. These big hunting lizards can change colors to hide perfectly. Sometimes, when I am walking beyond our village, I think I see one. Only for a moment. I hear rustling branches or a crunch on the rocky ground, but I find no trace. When winter comes, the snow will show their tracks. Warn all the dragons of the dwire danger, one more time. Especially the younger ones, since they are more likely to listen."

Jardor nodded. "We will find a way to deal with dwire. But there isss another problem. The dragons are restless. Everything isss new. We need game practices to give them something we know."

Drakor thumped him on the back. "*You* think more, too. Plan two half-days of fun. We can teach Lightning Swords on the pebble beach. Since the lake isss not frozen, we can use the meadow for Slam. Dragons can practice tail strikes using a ball, instead of the disc."

Jardor bowed and left.

Drakor flew down to the field below, at the edge of the forest. This flat field had solid rock just a claw length beneath the dirt, so trees could not grow. It would be perfect for Slam practice! Small, toothy lizards cropped the grasses at night and hid by day. He called them smidgers, after the lizards of their island. But these lizards could camouflage, like the still unseen dwire, so they were hard to catch.

Drakor peered into the forest. Twigs bent as invisible lizards leapt within trees, rapidly changing colors as they moved. Then something fell to the ground. He saw the odd sparkle of an oily, black eye. As the lizard died, the perfectly camouflaged body became visible, turning a splotchy brown.

Drakor grabbed the lizard, took a small bite, and spat it out. His mouth went numb. The bitter taste and numbing effect probably meant it was poisonous. Were dwire also poisonous? How many were in a pack, and when would they attack?

Drakor flew back to the village through a bright blue sky. He snapped his tail in surprise as cold drops spattered against his wings and slid down his scales. With frequent rain, new mushrooms popped up daily. Some tested toxic, but the edible mushrooms were dried and stored.

Drakor landed near Jardor. "That sun shower was short."

Jardor shrugged his wings. "It was long enough to clean the air."

Drakor flicked his tail nervously. "Will snow fall as often as this rain? We built our new dens with taller, steeper roofs to shed the snow. Are they steep enough? Or will snow pile up until the roofs collapse under the weight?"

Jardor took a long look at his friend. "You are doing everything you can. Worrying will not change what happens, but we could change the Slam field."

Drakor raised one eye ridge. "When did you get so

wise? And yes, that field isss still too rocky."

He assigned dragonlets to clear the field of the biggest rocks, under the protective watch of two dragon-dams.

As the sun sank lower, Drakor flew to the foothills. He collected roundish, fist-sized stones to carve into balls for the Slam game practices. Gathering stones also gave him a chance to explore, poking among rocks and hunting for secret caves.

The sky suddenly darkened, and ice-cold rain pelted the ground. Then, as fast as they came, the clouds disappeared. Evening sunlight turned the entire rain-drenched sky into a parade of rainbow colors, all with a reddish tinge. Each new, vivid color melted into the next. Blue-violet flowed into red-violet, then rose. Next was tangerine, which turned golden.

Drakor stood rooted to the ground as the sky colors changed. Indigo blue became purple, then black, and bright stars appeared. Orm, his artistic octopus friend, would love this! He straightened his wings. Scree said that what would be, would be, and then she would fix it. Well, there was beauty in this New World, and they would solve the new problems.

* * *

Drakor woke at dawn as orange light filled his den. He checked the magnetic lines for weather warnings and smiled. This was a perfect day for practice games. He signaled Jardor to sound the drum.

Soon, the Field-Slam practice began. Ten rough rocks served as goal-stones, while piles of roundish rocks served as game-stones. But their true game-stone was a sparkling blue disc that slid across ice.

Cranart pointed. "Form ten lines. Take turns hitting a game-stone ball with tail strikes, and aim for the goal-stone."

Dragons quickly formed ten lines, laughing and exercising their long tails.

Drakor looked east. This field was another plus for their new home. There were no good places to play field-Slam on their island, where scruffy clumps of grass grew among the rocks and boulders. "Cranart, we should think about real summer games, not just practices. We could carve perfectly round balls and try different ball sizes. We could even make up new games!"

Cranart's eyes glowed. "Summer games!"

Drakor grinned and pushed off, climbing into the sky with a heavy sack that glowed bright in his mind. This held their precious magnetic lodestones. He landed near a group of dragons and gave stones to each pair. "I need these back after your practice."

The dragons bowed and left, flying toward the distant white line of the glacier. Drakor followed them with his eyes. Soon, thunder crackled and boomed as they practiced sculpting ice with lightning.

Next, Drakor found Jardor on the pebble beach, by the lake. The damp rocks squeaked beneath his feet, protesting the weight of a dragon. He eyed the enormous pile of branches and driftwood. It was enough for a bonfire! "At least that terrible storm was good for something. There isss more than enough wood for target practice."

Jardor nodded. "Plenty. We made a game of gathering wood." He lowered his voice. "But some of these dragonlets have never even made a lightning sword!"

Drakor studied the bouncy youngsters. "I can teach the beginners while you help the ones who can throw swords. I taught golden dragons to make lightning swords and play the sword game. Teaching ice dragons should be easier."

Jardor raised one eye ridge. "And what did you learn from the golden dragons?"

Drakor grinned. "You will be surprised." He raised his wings for silence. "Every ice dragon should know how to make and use lightning swords. There isss one very important rule: *NEVER* use a lightning sword to attack a dragon. Swords are *only* for games and defense. You may defend yourself or your clan from an attack by something like a dwire. These dangerous hunters live in the forest and are hard to see, because they change colors to camouflage."

The dragonlets rustled their small wings, turning their heads from side to side, peering into shadows.

Drakor raised his wings again. "The dwire could be anywhere. But we are ice dragons! Now, to learn *how* to make lightning swords, come with me. If you already know, Jardor will help you improve."

One dragon-dam stayed with each practice group, as extra protection for the youngsters.

Five dragonlets surrounded Drakor, jumping up and down, flexing their small wings and flicking their tails. These youngsters had more energy than a lightning storm! He tossed ten pieces of wood onto the beach. "First, watch carefully. Then I will teach you."

Drakor flicked his claws out and a glowing pearl appeared. This grew quickly, twisting taller. In the blink of an eye, he held a bright sword. Within moments, he grew and threw ten lightning swords. Each one hit the target. Orange flames sprouted like odd flowers on the beach. Smoke drifted with the wind, carrying scents of different woods.

Dragonlets stared at the flames with huge eyes.

"An ice dragon should be able to hit any target. First, stand still and close your eyes. Feel the magnetic lines around us. Look for ones that wriggle."

Five dragons closed their eyes, bouncing in place with the boundless energy of the very young. Apparently, "still" was not an option.

"Now, open your eyes. Point to the wriggling line. That isss a magnetic wrinkle."

A young dragon squinted into the sky, struggling to keep both eyes open while he searched with inner sight. He pointed. "There!"

Drakor smiled. "Well done. Now, find ten more magnetic wrinkles. Then we will work on energy pearls."

Shadows shifted as the sun moved across a cloudless sky. "Time for a break!"

They plopped down and devoured their snacks. Then every set of eyes fastened on Drakor. He assigned a target for each dragonlet. "Find a magnetic wrinkle near your target. Now, feel the energy in the sky. Pull this into your open hand."

Minutes later, each dragon held a glowing pearl, an energy ball that hovered just above their claws.

Drakor nodded. "Pull in more sky energy. Grow your lightning ball."

Soon each dragonlet held blinding light that twisted wildly, reaching for the sky. Their eyes glowed with excitement that nearly matched the energy they held.

"Find a magnetic wrinkle near your target. Wait for the wrinkle to move over the target. Then throw the lightning. It will be drawn to the wrinkle."

Four swords hit the rocky beach, missing the wood. The fifth sword caught the edge of a log, which smoked.

Jardor stopped by near the end of practice, as their small wings began to droop.

Drakor whistled a halt. "Well done. Meet here tomorrow, same time."

Jardor pointed toward the burnt wood. "They learn fast."

Drakor grinned. "They are made of energy, so it isss easy to control energy. We need every set of claws ready to defend. I found large paw prints near our village, and they were *not* made by dragons."

CHAPTER 9: MIND QUEST

The sea reflected the flaming reds and orange of sunset. Waves clawed up the sides of the skiff, slipped through the railing, and washed across the deck. Arak adjusted the tiller and tied it off, taking a short break from steering. He kept his long wings furled as cold, salty wind knifed into him.

Arak shared a joyous grin with his long-time crewmates. He wiped cold sea spray off his golden scales and shouted above the wind, "We're making good time!" The skiff was their floating home. This time it carried four golden dragons, two small octopi, and three ice dragons.

Taron walked carefully on the slippery wood, with his golden wings folded tight against his back. His grin was as fierce as the sky. "This is *perfect!*"

Dorali flicked her golden tail up and down, in a perfect rhythm. "There's nothing else like it. I could stay here forever."

Slanting rays sparkled off Karoon's golden scales. He wrapped a line around the cleat and made neat coils with the remaining rope. "It *is* perfect. I feel completely of this world, like I'm living inside both sea and sky."

The other dragons turned as one to stare with wide eyes.

Arak clapped Karoon on the back. "Now you understand."

Dorali grinned. "That's *exactly* how it feels." She put her hands out, claws back, in the ice dragon way.

Karoon smoothly met her hands, claws back. He gazed into her eyes as if they were the only two dragons in the world.

Arak smiled. Dorali stood tall and proud, no longer trying to hide her scars from the world. Karoon had grown from a bully into a solid dragon, and Dorali's persistent suitor. Would she accept him as her mate?

Scree rested in a water-filled tub that was bolted to the deck. She colored her head and mantle to match the evening sky, while her arms became rolling sunset waves. "Sky and sea connect beautifully . . ."

Arak finished, ". . . like dragons and octopi." He stared out at the waves, which rippled up and down as far as the eye could see. "This surface is forever in motion, as if the sea itself is alive."

Scree nodded. "The sea *is* alive. Often peaceful,

sometimes dangerous, always lovely."

Suddenly, the air felt lighter. This was a severe weather warning! Arak closed his eyes and concentrated on the magnetic lines. They sparkled like a field of fireflies on a warm summer evening. Fierce storms were brewing, but where? "Taron, take over while I check the hold." He secretly signed, "I need to check to the north."

Taron looked him in the eye as he secretly signed, "Don't travel too far. Nobody knows what would happen if you abandon your body for too long."

Arak clapped his friend on the shoulder. "I'll be careful."

As a dragonlet, Arak had quested for hours in trance, his body limp. He even forgot to eat! When he mind-traveled, he saw what was really there; the adventure drew him on and on. No one knew why Arak stayed in trance, lost to the world, so he was bullied as a worthless "Dreamer". But Taron stuck by him, and now his friend was one of the very few who knew about this secret gift.

As Arak turned to leave, Taron reminded him, "Return soon."

Arak nodded. His friend understood the dangerous lure of this gift, even though Arak was the only dragon who could actually explore while in trance. He flung open the hatch and dropped down to the floor, landing lightly on the balls of his feet.

Sunset glowed down through a crystal cone set in the deck. This caught the sky and sent it below, filled the hold with fiery light. The walls glowed with aqua light from Orm's fungi, as if the sea had flowed in through the hull.

Golden dragons were all moving to the New World, so their only skiff was packed full for each voyage.

Dragons took turns crammed into a dark hold. Now, the crystal cone and glowing walls added welcome light. But this trip was different. They were traveling north along the coast to return their three ice dragon guests. With so few travelers, Arak could have privacy while he mind-traveled.

He made a quick check for leaks, feeling the walls for dampness while looking for warped boards or dark water stains. Arak sighed with relief. No leaks. Then he closed the overhead door, sat down, and gazed into his aquamarine trance-stone. His body went limp as his trance-mind rose up.

The skiff fell away and he sped north, questing.

* * *

When Arak's mind returned to his body, he woke to a darker hold. He stashed his globe and quickly climbed out. The fiery skies had changed as the sun slipped away. Evening waves reflecting a later sunset, gleaming like precious copper.

Arak quietly told Taron, "There's a powerful storm not far to the north. We must head for shore now. We're not too far from that cove you found."

Taron nodded, turning the tiller. "Weather's unpredictable at sea, and even more since those volcanoes erupted."

Stars appeared just as they reached the cove. Then storm clouds raced across the sky, hiding these lights.

Taron eyed the thick, dark clouds and thumped his tail with satisfaction. "We made it here just in time."

Arak looked over the side of the skiff, where flashes from glowing sea life lit the waves. "The sky's dark, but the sea sparkles. Let's anchor for the night and set crab traps."

Scree signed, "I need to stretch my arms in the sea. Orm and I can hunt and make another fish survey." She clambered out of her tub and slipped across the cold, wet deck, dragging a mesh bag.

Scree flattened her body, slid under the railing, and formed her head into a point. She dove straight down, parting the sea without a splash.

Orm followed close behind. He fell overboard in his usual way, sending up a small wave.

Arak flicked his tail nervously as his friends disappeared below the waves. They were armed and clever, but new territories had new dangers. He'd feel much better when Scree and Orm were safely back on board.

*   *   *

Scree turned white with shock as she hit the water. "It's colder here than last year."

Orm turned black and covered his body with lacy white snowflakes. "Definitely." Then they twirled down together.

Scree adjusted the mirrors in her skin cells to catch the dwindling light. She pointed up toward the surface. "You always make waves."

He grinned. "Just like you."

Scree laughed. "How?"

"I change the sea, if only for a moment. Your waves change the pod and the clan."

Scree pointed to the anemones around her mantle. "You change the pod with your farms and inventions." Her necklace of living flowers glowed in violet and rose, while Orm's anemones glowed in bright teal and orange.

Did this light help Orm enjoy his visits to the dangerous depths?

Scree had often explored the abyss, alone, bringing food to attract glowing fish and see by their light. Now she could bring her own light to better join this unique world.

Darkness closed in around her as they sank deeper into the sea, and the flowers seemed to glow brighter. Scree grinned. This could start a new fashion! Anemones were as beautiful as the abalone armbands the octopus dancers wore. Imagine dancing in the dark at a New Moon Festival while glowing with sea life.

As they drew near the seafloor, Scree's eyes bulged and she pointed. "Look!"

A ghostly arm reached down through the frigid water. The sea icicle stretched longer and longer until a twisted claw touched bottom. Then a frosty line raced along the dark seafloor. Starfish and sea urchins scattered frantically, but the ice ran faster. Sparkling fur sped across the floor and caught them. Many died in this crystal path of death.

Scree hovered above the icy ground. "Tarm spoke of this. These crystals are far colder than normal ice."

Orm stared. "Tarm, the giant squid? He's right. We need a safer place to land."

They pulsed south, keeping one eye pointed toward the dangerous brinicle.

Scree swiveled her other eye in all directions, hunting. "I feel the clicking of crabs, but there aren't many fish talking. Where are they?"

"Scree, even in this cold I can check chemicals, and the ones here aren't dangerous to fish."

Scree nodded. "We'll need to follow the fish route to find the place where they disappear. Then we can learn what's happening."

Hours later, Scree and Orm pulsed back to the skiff. They tied their catch bags to ropes that hung down the stern, into the sea. Then Scree pulled a cord that rang the bell, announcing their return. They could climb up the octopus ladder that was fastened to the side, but riding up was much faster.

Arak lowered buckets and pulled them up, one at a time. He sighed with relief when they were both safely aboard. "Welcome back!" Then he glanced over the stern. "What did you find?"

"Pink sea cucumbers and red crabs. And it's colder than ever. Deadly frost hunts along the seafloor."

*   *   *

Dawn painted both sea and sky in glowing shades of amber. Arak held the tiller and skiff-flew north, plunging across leftover storm waves. His eyes were drawn to the flaming colors of another spectacular sunrise. "It's brighter than ever!"

Dorali nodded. "Ever since the odd green skies disappeared, all we see are reds and orange. This change must be from the volcanoes, but I miss the purple and rose colors."

A white dragonlet walked over to Dorali, automatically lifting her feet to anticipate the rising deck.

Dorali nodded approvingly. "You still have your sea legs."

Jordana smiled shyly. "I skiff-flew before I could run. I love the sea." The youngster trembled and looked down at the deck. "I hope I can visit, when my wings grow longer and I can fly . . . Will you remember me?"

Dorali wrapped her wings around Jordana. "No one will ever forget you. What's really bothering you?"

Jordana flicked her tail nervously and whispered, "I have always lived with golden dragons. I do not know ice dragons. Will I act right? Will they like me?"

Dorali sighed. "I do understand. It's hard to feel different. You learned our ways easily, so you'll learn the ways of ice dragons. But it's alright if a part of you is always a bit different. A field with only one kind of flower would be boring."

A smile lit her face like lightning within clouds. "Flower?" She giggled. "I am not a flower."

Dorali touched foreheads with the youngster. "You're unique, and I'll miss you more than you know."

Jordana straightened her small wings. "As soon as I can fly, I *will* find a way to visit."

The skiff jerked suddenly, caught by an unexpected wave. Jordana's dam grabbed the railing in a death grip and stared to the west, flicking her long white tail uneasily. There was nothing to see but star-lit water.

Arak moved closer to the dam. "Don't worry. We're skiff-flying along the coast, close enough to find shelter if we need to outrun a storm. We'll get you safely home in another day or two."

The dragon-dam turned to face Arak but kept a tight grip on the railing. "I have never seen our new home."

He pointed northwest. "Your village is near an old volcano, and there's a lake with huge fish. I think you'll like it."

Scree pulled up higher in her tub and peered at the waves. "It's the season for squid journeys, so we could meet these giants again."

Orm shuddered as he glanced overboard from his tub. "I'd prefer a trip without that particular pleasure."

Taron flicked his tail nervously. "So would I."

Dorali set a tray down on a low table, and every nose turned toward the scented steam.

"Hot chocolate!"

She grinned. "Grab a mug. This wind speeds our journey, but it steals the warmth." She gave small cups to Scree and Orm before taking her own mug.

Just then, two long, reddish brown snakes rose up from the sea and slithered over the railing. The skiff shook as if caught in a sudden storm.

Dragons grabbed for anything solid as the skiff tilted back and forth. Hot chocolate spilled onto the deck, adding a sweet scent to the smells of polished wood and seawater.

A huge yellow eye glowed up through the water. Then another. Two giant squid surfaced, each longer than the skiff.

Arak held tight to the rigging as the skiff pitched wildly. Why did their monstrous friends need to be so dangerously playful? Fortunately, the hold was heavily weighted with rocks. This ballast and the deep keel gave the dragon skiff great stability, to keep it from flipping over.

The ice dragons seemed to turn a whiter shade of snow, and their eyes were huge.

Arak signed to Scree, "Our dragon guests have never seen anything bigger than their own kind."

Scree rolled her eyes. "How could they? *Nothing* on land is bigger than an ice dragon!" She climbed up a ramp arm over arm, using her suction cups, and hung three arms over the side. Scree made a series of red and yellow spots on her skin, her version of squid lights. "Veera and Tarm. How good to see you. How do you find us?"

Three of Scree's arms made spots as she spoke with the squid, while two more arms translated the spot-words for dragons and Orm.

Veera grinned while yellow and red lights flashed along her speaking arms. "Your floating island is easy to find. The sea is full of eyes." The squid's long mantle flushed with subtle colors.

Scree focused one eye on Veera's intended light message. Her other eye tracked the squid's posture and mantle colors. Veera was laughing!

Scree made more message spots. "The sea is full of squid eyes?"

Veera's arms sparkled with lights. "Squid are everywhere. The sea is our home. An ancient shark sends you a message."

"You didn't eat it?"

Veera shook her head. "Squid don't eat this shark. It's too interesting and wise, like you."

"I'm interesting and wise?"

"You're interesting. I'm not sure about wise." Veera's mantle flushed with colors.

Scree matched these colors on her own body, joining the squid's laughter.

Veera's entire body turned shock-white for a split second. "You understood! Perhaps you are wise, too."

Scree shrugged her octopus shoulders in a dragonly way. "Wisdom is difficult to judge. What did the shark say?"

"The seafloor is shaking in the east, so another island is ready to hatch. This shark has studied the night sky for many generations of squid. A huge star-stone is coming. It may hit the sea or start fires on land. Warn your sky-swimmer friends."

Scree twirled her arms nervously. How could they prepare for such things? "Please thank him for the warning. What have *you* learned?"

Veera flashed her lights to answer. "Sunsets are brighter, like a swarm of red krill. The world is colder. Some fish died when the volcanoes exploded. But something new is killing the fish, and we don't know what. Tell us when you find it. Also, squid are hunting beyond the abyss. We reminded them of the treaty, but be wary."

Scree straightened her arms. "Warn *them* to be wary. If squid attack, we'll capture them and make them glow."

Tarm rippled with laugh colors. "That's a fate worse than death. The ice is growing again, instead of breaking apart. I miss riding the thunder waves, when ice mountains fall into the sea."

Veera gave a ferocious grin, a fearsome sight. "It's time for us to hunt." She flashed red and yellow lights in the traditional squid greeting-farewell.

Scree answered with bright red and yellow spots, "May you surf the tangled currents of the sea forever."

Arak waved farewell as the squid disappeared. "Scree, I'm glad you're aboard to talk with them."

Scree nodded. "Giant squid are interesting. They glow brightly through life. But we should make more language skins in case they visit when I'm not aboard."

Arak laughed. "Yes. But, somehow, they always

seem to know when *you* are here."

Zardan, Drakor's sire, was staring down into the sea. "I wish I could see deeper."

Arak nodded. "I do, too. An entire world is hidden beneath these waves. It's the realm of octopi and giant squid."

The next day, dawn burned with golden flames. Arak gazed at the fiery sea, awash with reflected sky colors. "I love how the sea captures the sky. Taron, we should reach the ice dragon shore in a day or two, but we need more fresh water *now*."

Taron pointed northwest. "We can anchor in that cove with the stream."

Arak stretched and folded his wings. "There are clams in the sea and wild carrots in the meadow. Let's gather food for the welcome feast."

An hour later, they anchored near the shore. This cove had towering, black rock islands and impressive tides. Arak set three storm anchors to keep the skiff from crashing against the rocks. He signed to Scree and Orm, "Could you hunt on the reef?"

Scree grabbed her mesh bag. "I could use the exercise. Orm, we can do another fish survey."

Orm nodded. "The tide's still flowing out and should turn back in a couple hours. Perfect."

They slipped overboard together.

* * *

Scree relaxed into the pull of the bitterly cold current, and was swiftly carried offshore. When the current lost its strength, she pulsed to the rocky reef with Orm.

This place was eerily quiet, with no sounds to paint a picture of the reef's residents. Scree poked between rocks and checked for movement beneath the sand. She spied the beady black eyes of a stone crab, hidden beneath the ledge. She curled her arms, ready to strike.

The eye-skin behind her head caught a streak of blue.

As Scree whipped around, a wave of water rushed over her. Suddenly, she was in the jaws of a shark! Her intelligent arms sprang into action, pushing into the shark's gills on both sides of its head.

The shark shook its head violently from side to side, trying to shake her arms loose. It couldn't breathe. Scree pushed her arms deeper into the gills, denying it new oxygen-water.

Desperate to breathe, the shark released her.

Scree jerked her arms out of the gills. She shot ink directly into the shark's face, confusing its sense of smell. Then, hidden by this dark cloud, she jetted away.

Scree squeezed her boneless body partway under a rock. Her skin instantly crumpled to match, turning gray with crusty pink patches of algae. In the blink of an eye she disappeared in plain sight. She held as still as the rock she resembled, as still as death.

The shark shook its head, trying to clear out the ink. Then it prodded the reef with its pointed nose, peering beneath rocks, searching. Scree stopped sucking water in through her siphon as she held her breath.

The shark was a sleek cylinder, perfectly built for speed. It swam in tight circles around the hidden prey, searching. But all it caught was the light that gleamed on its bright, silvery sides. Finally, the shark tore away, thrashing its tail angrily.

A nearby rock morphed into an octopus. Orm smoothed his skin and squirted over. "Scree, that was too close."

The Scree-rock took a deep breath, changed back, and twined arms with her mate. "Yes. And too fast. There was no time for a ride. That was a young mako shark, the fastest of them all! They can leap a dragon's length out of the sea."

Orm rolled his eyes. "Really? You want to ride *another* shark? Riding the waves would be safer, and looks like just as much fun."

Scree's eyes grew brighter. "Orm! You just said surfing was fun!"

Orm grinned. "Not precisely. Just *as much* fun."

Scree turned toward the distant shore. Waves crashed, slipped back, and crashed again, with this eternal song. "When we left our home, we also left the land of the golden dragons. You said that if our flying friends moved here too, we'd fly the waves together to celebrate."

Orm shuddered. "True."

Scree stroked his arm gently. "This is the perfect place. We'll start with small waves. Then we can shoot through the tunnels!"

Orm gave a half smile. "Yay."

Scree covered her skin with cresting waves in shades of happy-green. "After we hunt, we can tie our bags to the skiff and still have time to surf the sea."

Orm turned both eyes toward the distant, crashing shore. "What will be, will be. First, we hunt."

Scree nodded. "And do a quick fish survey. Then we can hunt up another shark to ride."

Orm rolled his eyes.

Scree laughed. "We'll see Drakor soon. I wonder how he's doing."

CHAPTER 10: PLAYING WITH FIRE

Drakor soared high on the currents, circling, searching the sea below. Afternoon rays slanted across the waves, adding a golden glow. He shivered as wispy clouds streamed across his wings, washing them in cold, wet air. When would they arrive?

Drakor tasted the salty air, recalling his journeys across sea and sky. He smiled with the memories and added two words to his favorite undersea greeting: "May you surf the currents of the sea *and sky* forever."

A small, silvery-white fin appeared on the horizon.

Drakor snapped his tail as it grew into a huge, triangle skiff-wing, flying across the waves toward the shore. The skiff slowed as it entered the cove, a protected circle of sea that was nearly surrounded by the rocky shore. A narrow, wooden dock reached out from the land, waiting.

Drakor dove straight down and landed beside Jardor. "The dragons are here! Sound the drum!"

BOOOM! BOOOM! BOOOM! The dragon-sized drum thundered three times, rumbling through Drakor's body. White wings filled the sky like early snow as ice dragons flocked to the shore. The triple beat announced the arrival of guests and, soon, a welcome feast. No dragon ignored this signal!

Remnants of their crude shelters dotted the rocky beach. These had been hastily made from anything they could scavenge. The largest boulders remained, but death waves stole the rest. These remnants marked the spot where the clan landed after that long, terrible flight.

Drakor shuddered at the memory. His wings felt like burning ice, growing heavier with each stroke. But the burden of leading the clan into the unknown was heavier still.

He had shocked the dragons by defeating Mardor, their long-time leader. Then he led the disbelieving clan away from their doomed island, while his wounds still bled from the challenge fight. He followed the stars and magnetic lines, monitoring their position and storms. They flew high in the wind-stream, miles above the ground, safely above most storms. Flying with the wind shortened their time, but it was bitterly cold, well below freezing.

Drakor chose the fastest route, but their flight to the New World was still dangerously long, even for ice dragons. And there was no place to stop and rest.

Drakor flew point, trying to prove his worth; a series of "V" formations spread out behind him. Breaking the sky-trail was tiring work, but this made an easier path for those who followed. Despite the bitter cold, his muscles burned with the strain. When his wing strokes faltered, Jardor moved up beside him to take his place. Drakor nodded and slipped back, grateful for the reprieve.

The dragons flew nonstop, hour after hour. Dragonlords took turns carrying the heavy, flightless dragonlets in slings. They worked in groups of four, trading off in the sky as they flew.

The ice dragons left their island home just before dawn. They snacked while flying and stretched their arms back again, streamlined to fly faster. The dragons flew all that day and through the night. The sun rose again, and still they flew! In all their legends, dragons had never flown so far without stopping.

Drakor was exhausted and half-frozen, flying as if dead. The sea below was a flat, gray-green circle, and they were always in the center. This never-changing view numbed his mind while frost numbed his body.

Then the beach appeared. This solid surface was more glorious than a feast! They could finally land.

Drakor snapped out of his reverie when the skiff reached the dock. The shore had a salty-dead smell, the eternal scent of the sea, which triggered memories of skiff-flying with friends.

Arak, his golden dragon friend, tossed sausage-shaped cushions over the side. This protected both skiff and dock as he managed a soft landing. He leapt onto the pier and fastened ropes around pillars, securing the skiff. He called to the crew, assigning watch duty.

Jordana walked down the narrow plank from skiff to dock, bouncing cheerfully as it bent beneath her, eyes bright with interest. The dam followed close behind, sighing with relief when she stepped onto solid land. Then she stumbled.

Dorali caught her arm. "Your legs are still walking with the sea, moving with the waves. Take small steps. You'll soon have your land legs."

Drakor stared at a dragon flying from the skiff to the shore. His crippled sire was flying!

Zardan landed gracefully beside him. He touched foreheads in the respectful manner of golden dragons. "It isss good to be back."

Drakor's eyes glistened with emotion as a tragic memory met overwhelming happiness. He owed so much to the golden dragons, and to Scree. Years ago, Zardan was buried in an avalanche. Drakor was just a small dragonlet, but he kept digging until he freed his sire from the snow and rocks.

But Zardan was crippled, and the clan considered him a useless burden. Unable to fly, he would have died with their island when the Volcano erupted. Instead, Drakor's friends saved and healed his sire. Zardan once again had the freedom of the skies!

Merika greeted Zardan. Then she met Drakor's eyes. "This isss why I must leave, to learn the healing magic."

Drakor nodded. "I know." He gazed at the skiff that brought his sire and clan members. Soon, this skiff would leave with the one friend he needed most. His tail drooped to the ground.

Arak landed and bowed respectfully to the leader. When Drakor bowed back, dragons rustled their wings in irritation. Some whispered loudly that the leader of ice dragons, the biggest dragons of all, should never bow to anyone!

Arak raised one eye ridge.

Drakor signed silently, "They do not fully appreciate what you have done for us, and I am not quite the leader they expect."

A short glide away, a cluster of huge dragon-lords stood wing-to-wing, watching. These were the oldest ice dragons, nearly twice Arak's size and all scarred from fights. Mardor was the biggest of them all. He stood tall and proud with wings stiffly folded, as if he was carved from ice.

Arak nodded pleasantly to the group. The dragons ignored him except for Mardor, who narrowed his eyes and glared back. Arak said quietly, "He really hates me."

Drakor flicked his tail. "Yes. He knows you helped me survive. But he hates me more. I took away what he loves most, his power. His anger isss like a Volcano, ready to explode."

Arak shuddered. "Do you ever wish Mardor had *not* survived the flight here?"

Drakor shook his head. "I am the leader and he isss a member of the clan. I do not want him hurt, but I do not think he feels the same about me." He studied the hulking figure. "He isss the biggest dragon ever, and he isss looking for a way to challenge me. I do not know if I can win another fight."

Arak cocked his head sideways. "But you do have a

plan?"

Drakor's eyes brightened and he gave a deep, booming laugh. "Yes. You and Scree taught me that much." He nodded toward the skiff, feeling a strong magnetic pull. "You brought the rest of our lodestones?"

Arak grinned and clapped him on the back, in the rough, ice dragon way. "Yes. You need them for a proper Winter Festival." Arak pulled a clear quartz jar from his sack, filled with blue-green powder. "This gift is from Arafine, from one leader to another. It's more of the crushed copper rock from our mine."

Arak took a second jar from his sack. Six-sided, metallic gray crystals showed through the clear sides. "This is from me. I struck a rare vein of selenium crystals. They burn true blue, like a clear winter sky. Use this for a special fire."

Drakor cradled both jars. "These are perfect! Blue isss the color of freedom." He handed Arak a box carved from fragrant wood. "I too have been playing with fire, and not just about fights."

Arak stared at the lid. "The whorl in this wood grain looks like a flying dragon! Dorali's right. Your art always includes something natural." He slid the lid off and peered inside. "What's this?"

Drakor grinned. "Iron filings, from a star-stone in the ice sheet. These will add golden sparks to your fire, the color of your scales."

Arak's eyes grew wide. "Thank you! I've never found a star-stone. If you find any more, they'd make great trade items."

Drakor looked toward the distant glacier. "These star-stones are pure iron, and dark, so the sun heats the stones.

They melt the ice, sink into it, and are hidden below the surface. We hunt for them with magnetic sight."

Dorali joined them. She gave Drakor a small bag and signed, "If you must fight, chew three of these candies first. Orm helped. He says it's more efficient than the tea you drank before your last fight."

Drakor opened the bag and his eyes lit up. Chocolate! Then his nose wrinkled at the unexpectedly sharp scent. He gave a lopsided grin. "Chocolate candy with bitter herbs. Only Orm could think of this. Thank him for me."

Dorali shook her head. "You can thank him yourself. Scree and Orm are aboard."

Drakor's eyes glowed. "I can visit after the feast. I have missed all of you!" He raised his wings high and waited, making sure he had everyone's attention. Then he bowed to the golden dragons. "This feast celebrates the return of our ice dragons. Thank you for bringing them safely home. Now, fill the feasting table!"

Drakor grinned as dragons hurried to comply. This was the one command he could give and expect instant obedience, like a proper leader.

The rough table was on a high ridge within sight of shore. It was hastily assembled from large stones fitted between boulders. But the plates, bowls, and platters were newly carved from stone or wood.

Ice dragons brought out their traditional foods first. There were platters piled high with fish and huge bowls of colorful lichen salads topped with creamy pine nuts. Next were New World treats: nuts mixed with wild green apples and bright red cranberries. Golden mushrooms were sliced thin and paired with small lake clams.

Huge wooden buckets sat on the stony ground by the

far end of the table. Most held cold stream water, but five had spiced, honey-sweetened, Sassafras root drink. This was their favorite New World beverage.

Golden dragons placed their contributions on the table. Three platters were piled high with snow crabs, caught during their last stop. A bowl with golden-brown mushrooms was decorated with sprigs of rosemary and mint. Five platters held scraped wild carrots in their many colors: magenta, yellow, white, and the more common deep purple. These carrots were arranged in colorful patterns. One platter had a sunburst design, one had a fanciful snowflake pattern, and three had colorful patterns of jagged lightning.

Drakor flicked his tail happily. He had missed the artistic feasting of golden dragons.

Arak added serving plates with food from Scree and Orm. These had clams, crab claws, and seaweed in the tastiest colors: gold, red, and purple.

Tempting aromas filled the air. Many of Drakor's age-mates opened their wings wide, making an arched display. This signaled an acceptance of change, of their new home, and of Drakor as leader.

Arak nodded toward the stretched wings.

Drakor smiled sadly. "The younger dragons accept me and our new home, but they remember only the hungry years on our island. For them, this food isss reason enough to move. But my sire taught me our legends and shared stories from his youth. I know what the older dragons miss so much. They miss the good memories and the hope for a better future, in the home of our ancestors. And now that hope isss gone."

Drakor turned to the waiting crowd and raised his

wings high. "Today, we feast on food from land and sea! Golden dragons also brought chocolates, one for each of us, as a guest gift." He ceremoniously added this bowl to the center of the table and nodded to his second-in-command.

Jardor struck the drum three times.

Dragons filed past the feasting table, commenting on the variety of food and artistic displays. Then they lined up at the head of the table on each side, grinning, snapping their tails.

As the leader, Drakor went first. His in-commands were next, and the guests. Then the rest of the dragons filed past the food, carefully selecting their proper portion from the bowls and platters. After years of hunger, this habit was deeply ingrained.

When the plates were empty and stacked, Drakor raised his wings. "It isss time to trade."

Silent circles formed, with the tallest dragons standing in the back while those in the closest rings sat on the ground. Drakor, Arak, and Dorali were in the center, surrounded by an audience that was as still as ice, watching.

Arak and Dorali spread their items across the stony ground. There were large sacks with starchy tubers, colorful carrots, or salty red seaweed. Next were five small jars of golden honey, a bowl filled with gleaming pearls, and chocolate.

Drakor smiled. "That isss even more food than I had hoped for." He pointed to the pearls. "And Orm has been busy."

A young dragon whispered loudly, "Honey and chocolate!"

Ice dragons placed items opposite the golden dragon items. First were three emerald-green armbands that sparkled brighter than diamonds. These were carved from a rare mass of solid garnet, and they matched the green rim on Dorali's golden scales.

Arak eyed the arm bands. "It's the exact shade of our green lightning."

Drakor nodded. "We use blue, you use green. If an ice dragon-lady accepts blue lightning from a dragon-lord, they are mated for life."

Ice dragons added three piles of Volcano stones that sparkled in the afternoon light: emerald-green, ruby-red, and sapphire-blue. Some of these gems were larger than a dragon's fist! Next were five agate bowls that were cleverly carved, using the natural rainbow swirls to suggest dragons. These bowls were polished as smooth as melting ice. Smoked fish fillets were piled high. These were wrapped in hemp, and a magnet for dragon noses. Then came small gemstone jars, carved thin to be light.

Arak's eyes glowed as the fish skins were stacked high. "They're huge, perfect for skiff-wings. I'd like to trade first for all three of the green arm bands. Taron and I have traveled non-stop, moving our clan to the New World. These bands will help our mates remember us."

Drakor smiled. "And the third arm band?"

Arak glanced toward the skiff. "I have a friend who will want this."

Drakor's smile grew into a broad grin. "I think I know this dragon. For one jar of honey, you can have all three. What do you want for that chocolate?"

"Half of the smoked fish and all the fish skins."

Arak and Drakor made the exchange.

Ice dragons watched with eager eyes while whispering, "Chocolate!"

Dorali held each of the agate bowls up to the sun, one at a time. Light glowed through them in cheerful colors, like earth rainbows. "These are beautiful. Our clan should see your art. What do you want for them?"

Dragons grinned at the compliment while Drakor named the barter price.

They traded the small gemstone jars for pearls. "Scree will want these for the Healers."

Trading continued, like a game, until all the items had swapped sides.

Arak bowed formally. "The items we traded for will be carried home and shared." He looked from the impressive pile on his side to the much smaller pile on Drakor's side. He secretly signed, "You had many more items, yet the exchange was even. You worked that out perfectly."

Drakor smiled. "Your items are rare and precious. This has been an excellent exchange." He silently signed, "In truth, I owe you more than I could ever give. And so does the clan." He tilted his head toward Mardor's dark scowl. "Though some dragons would not agree."

The air grew cooler as the sun sank low in the sky. Drakor assigned dragons to carry Arak's items to the dock. By the time everything was loaded onto the skiff, a golden-orange sunset glowed along the western horizon.

Drakor raised his wings high. "It isss time to light the festival fire. Our new home isss rich in firewood. We light *this* fire to celebrate the safe arrival of our clan members. We also celebrate trade between ice dragons and golden dragons."

The clan was silent, staring at the logs that were piled high within a circle of rocks.

Drakor hid a satisfied smile. Their old island home had biting winds, with only a few stunted trees. There was little wood to burn. But this was a forested land, and fires were a new treat.

Drakor channeled the sky, sending a thin lightning sword into the wood pile. Tongues of flame blossomed and spread. Soon a warm fire blazed in yellows and orange, with bright red sparks. Then he tossed on branches from wild apple and birch trees, adding delicious aromas to the fire. Scented smoke and cheerful crackling filled the air. This was another new experience for the clan.

As the sun disappeared, the fire blazed brighter. Dragons leaned in, flaring their nostrils to catch the smoky, dragonny scents. Their eyes reflected the flames, glowing golden-gray.

Stars gleamed in the darkness. Golden curtains of light rippled and danced to an unheard song. Then glowing green ribbons swirled exuberantly across the night, like the flight paths of mating dragons. Drakor flicked his tail in surprise. Where did that thought come from?

He gave a secret signal to Jardor, and all his in-commands left. Minutes later they returned. Each carried a basket filled with old, weathered pinecones. The cones had a normal, piney smell but an odd, blue-green sheen.

Arak eyed the baskets. "Is this what I think it is?"

Drakor signed, "I soaked these cones in copper salts." He stretched his wings slowly, moving as if he was simply stiff, and grinned. Stretched wings were the new

114

sign for change.

Arak signed back, "Scree says that change must start somewhere. This should be interesting."

A dragon-dam pointed to the baskets. "That isss a lot of pinecones. What are they for?"

Drakor held a cone high. "Dragons play lightning sword games. Now we can also play fire games. These pinecones make colored fire, for a choosing game."

Dragons snapped their tails in excitement.

"A new game!"

"How do we play?"

Drakor began juggling three pinecones, a skill learned from his golden friend, Karoon. He smoothly added a fourth cone to his juggling routine. Dragon eyes gleamed as they followed the flying cones. "These pinecones burn with blue flame. I will give you a choice, and each of you will have one pinecone to show your choice. If you choose 'No', keep your cone. If most of you keep your cone, the fire will stay orange. That means 'No', and that isss what we will all do."

He stopped juggling, catching each cone as it fell. "If you choose 'Yes', toss your cone into the fire. If most of you toss your cone into the fire, the color will change to blue. This means most of you choose 'Yes', and that isss what we will *all* do."

Each dragon took one cone from a basket. Mardor glowered as he took his cone. Drakor nodded to himself. His nemesis was more than just a great fighter; he understood the seeds of change within this game. To a dragon like Mardor, this would be the most dangerous game.

When everyone held a cone, Drakor raised his wings

for silence. "It isss late. We could stop for the night, or stay longer and share legends. If you think we should *not* stay, choose 'No' and keep your cone. If you think we *should* stay and share legends, choose 'Yes' and toss your pinecone into the fire. If enough choose 'Yes', the fire will turn bright blue."

Mardor looked from dragon to dragon, shaking his head 'no' while shredding his pinecone. Some stared back at him with wide eyes while others scrunched their eye ridges, whispering, "Why?" His followers also wore puzzled expressions. But his strongest supporters nodded agreement and, when Mardor threw his shredded cone onto the ground, his cronies followed suit.

The rest of the dragons looked from their odd, greenish cones to the cheerful orange fire. Then a stream of pinecones flew through the air, landing neatly in the fire. Tendrils of blue flame sprouted and grew together, making a beautiful blue fire, the first the clan had ever seen.

This fire glowed like the blue lightning that ice dragons made to choose a mate. It was the color of the sky, of freedom. But this fire meant a new kind of freedom, to choose as a group, beyond the decision of the leader.

Drakor felt the warm glow of success all the way down to the tip of his tail. Just as he hoped, the lure of blue fire and starlit story-telling was too much to resist. Dragons wanted to play this new game, so Mardor had failed.

The seeds of change were planted. How would this change the clan?

CHAPTER 11: LEGENDS

Drakor could not quite hide his grin as he raised his wings exuberantly high. "You chose blue flames, for story-telling. Arak, would you share a legend?"

Arak walked to the fire and stretched tall. "The First Golden Dragon was born of Storm. He was made from the four elements of life: Fire, Water, Air, and Land." He spoke like a storm, loud and fierce, and his words rumbled through the darkness.

Dragons leaned forward, eyes glowing in the firelight.

"Storm covered our world, shaking it with terrible thunder. Storm was lonely, so he sent a red bolt of lightning through the rain-drenched sky. It burned the golden sand, melting a crater."

Arak poured golden sand onto the ground, gleaming in the firelight. He held a long branch of red coral, carved like jagged lightning, and swiftly struck the sand. At the same moment he tossed a handful of powder into the fire.

BOOM!!!

The ice dragons reared back.

Arak grinned. This explosive powder was a mix of sulfur, charcoal, and dried lizard poop.

"A golden dragon-lord leapt out of the crater. Each golden scale had a thin ruby edge that matched the red lightning. The dragon was created from air, rain-water, land, and lightning-fire. He flew as fast as the wind and danced with lightning to honor the Storm."

Arak wove one hand through the sky as if it was a flying dragon, swooping and spiraling. The dragon-shadows danced across the ground.

"But the dragon-lord was lonely." Arak let his wings droop while his tail sank to the ground. "So the Storm made a rare shaft of green lightning, the color of new spring leaves." He grabbed a jagged rod from his pouch, carved from rare, emerald-green jade. He threw this green lightning into the sand while again using the explosive powder to make thunder.

"A dragon-lady flew up from the crater. Each of her golden scales had an emerald rim, the color of green lightning. The dragons flew up together into the clouds and danced with the Storm."

Arak wove two hands in front of the fire, making large, winged shadows move across the ground. The shadow-dragons twirled up into darkness and disappeared.

"We are born of Storm. A dragon-lord chooses a mate in the Storm dances. He uses red metal powder, like the rim of his scale, to turn a lightning bolt green, like the rim of a dragon-lady scale. Then he tosses this green lightning to a dragon-lady. If she tosses it back, they're mated for life."

Taron stepped forward and gave him a large ceramic bowl. The hardened clay had swirls of blue and green, like the sea. Blue-green abalone pearls formed a pattern of cresting waves near the rim.

Drakor held the bowl high, turning so all could see. "A dragon-dam makes a nest bowl for her egg, following clan tradition. The egg must hatch in a nest that combines land, water, fire and air. The First Dragon was born of these four elements. Now all dragons are born within them. The nest bowl is made of clay, softened by water, and hardened by fire and air. Gemstones are added for special meaning. This ancient magic nurtures the dragonlet."

Dragon-ladies leaned forward for a closer look at the nest, murmuring approval.

Arak bowed. The audience snapped and thumped their tails in thunderous applause.

Drakor added his applause. When the noise finally died down, he raised his wings high. "Thank you, Arak! Now I will share the legend of the First Ice Dragon."

Drakor smiled. This legend was even older than the dragon-sized trees hidden deep in the forest. "The Volcano rose high above the ice. Lightning crackled through his hot, dark clouds and he ROARED!" Drakor threw his head back and roared, louder than thunder.

"White lightning struck the glacier again and again, carving the ancient ice into a solid white body." Drakor gathered energy on his claws and threw small lightning swords into the ground near his feet.

"Dragon scales covered the body like shattered ice on a frozen stream. A jagged ridge ran down the back. The Volcano melted long, smooth wings that flowed out from the ice body. He threw two bolts of black lightning and cut dark eyes into the head. His sculpture was complete, and lifeless."

Drakor crouched low and spread his wings wide across the ground, holding as still as an ice sculpture.

"Then the Volcano gathered white diamonds, made from blood-red fire deep inside his heart. These icy crystals held his fiery spirit. He ground them into sparkling dust and sprinkled this over his sculpture. Diamond dust settled into the rim of each white scale."

Drakor held up his massive, eight-sided diamond. This crystal gleamed with inner light, as if it was alive. Then he snapped his wings wide, springing to life with a gale of wind.

Dragons leaned into the wind from his wings.

"The dragon's scales sparkled and her dark eyes glowed with life. She drew in her first frozen breath, sprang into the sky, and flew high above the Volcano. Then she dove back through the dark clouds, flying faster than the wind. The First Dragon was made from the Volcano and ice, as fierce as burning lava and as wild as a winter storm."

Drakor bowed. The audience applauded with enthusiastic tail thumps. This was a story they all knew by heart but never tired of hearing.

Mardor raised his wing and then waited quietly for Drakor to call on him. "I, too, have a story to share."

Drakor studied the giant. He was never this polite. What was Mardor planning now? Warily, he nodded assent.

Mardor strode confidently to the center.

Drakor gritted his teeth when the clan was instantly silent for their former leader.

"This isss a legend we must never forget, of our three gem-colored lakes: ruby, moonstone-white, and turquoise." Mardor held up a large, polished stone as he mentioned each lake gem.

Drakor noted that the stones were of low quality, but the colors matched their old lakes perfectly. These gems had not been found in the New World, so they must be from their island. Mardor must have carried the heavy rocks on his long flight here. But were these legend-stones his personal treasure, or just part of his plan to win back power?

Mardor held his stones in the firelight, where they shone like sunlit lakes. Then he slipped them back into his sack.

"Long ago, the world grew colder. Ice Dragons left the Volcano. After many generations, our past was nearly forgotten."

Mardor held still, wings drooping and head bowed.

"Then the clan grew ill. One brave dragon left, flying north, seeking a way back to the Volcano who made them. Surely he would know how to heal them! The dragon-lord followed an ancient rumor. He searched for the secret path of three stones, each the size of three dragons."

Mardor snaked his head this way and that, as if searching.

"The dragon-lord found each worn stone. They barely showed above the waves, but were a much-needed place to rest. On the fourth day, he reached our beautiful Volcano Island and landed near three clear lakes."

Mardor put three polished quartz stones on the ground, matching the clear lakes.

"A deep voice sounded inside the dragon's head. 'Welcome home. Your journey was long, and your clan suffers. I will create healing waters.' Then the Volcano breathed his smoky breath across the lakes. The first lake turned ruby red, like Volcano blood, like ice dragon blood."

Mardor held his ruby gem high, and it winked in the firelight.

"The Volcano said, 'We share the same red blood. You have flown far and are exhausted. Drink of this lake.' The dragon-lord drank with a thirst beyond thirsts, and energy returned to his body."

"The second lake turned icy white, like our scales, but the water was warm like a dragon."

Mardor held up his shimmering moonstone.

"The Volcano spoke again. 'You are worried. Drink of this icy warmth. Ice dragons are made of fire and ice. You need both.' The dragon drank again and a deep calm filled his mind."

Mardor held up his turquoise stone.

"The third lake turned sky-blue. The Volcano said, 'I gave you wings, for the freedom of the sky. Drink and be healed of spirit.' The dragon drank the blue water and was filled with hope. He flew through the Volcano's smoky breath, spiraling with joy."

Mardor put his three colored gemstones on the ground, in the order of their lakes.

"Then the Volcano gave the dragon-lord one last gift. 'Gather the blue berries from the ice-flower plants. Carry them to your clan. Each dragon must eat three berries to heal. Then they may return here, to their true home.'"

Mardor stretched his arms to the east, as if reaching for his perfect home.

"The dragon-lord bowed and left. Three moons later, his clan followed the stones back to the Volcano, where they lived for generations in health and safety."

Mardor stood tall. "We must never forget our Volcano, our precious lakes, or our lovely home." He finished with an elegant bow.

Tails began thumping, and Drakor joined the applause. This was a well told story. Dragons were gazing to the east, eyes bright with memories, tails drooping. Drakor also missed their island, but he knew it was gone. Mardor had found another way to sow discontent. Did he miss their island as much as he missed his power?

Drakor raised his wings high. "Arak, thank you for bringing our dragons home. Tomorrow at sunrise, we feast! Then we will all return to our homes, and may the winds be with you."

He motioned to Arak and Dorali. "There isss something you must see, tonight, before you leave. Follow me."

They glided inland to a small meadow, where tiny yellow stars flashed.

Arak smiled at the sparkling display. Then his eyes grew wide. These fireflies were turning their lights on and off at exactly the same time, flashing together. "How do they manage to all flash at the same time?"

Drakor grinned. "I think this clan of fireflies could be a living aurora, connected by light, speaking with light."

Arak laughed. "That makes as much sense as anything else. I need to get back to the skiff."

Drakor turned his head toward the sea, feeling an instinctive pull. "I'll race you." He leapt into the sky, glided to the skiff, and landed neatly on deck. Moments later, Arak and Dorali landed beside him, laughing.

As soon as Drakor's claws touched the damp wood, his worries slipped away like the tide. Rolling waves and scents of the sea triggered happy memories, back to a time before the strain of being a new leader in a new land. Here were true friends who wanted him to succeed.

Drakor greeted his octopus friends by twining claw-to-arm. He spoke with fluid gestures, grinning with relief: he could still speak proper Octopus. That worried him while he taught this silent language to Merika. Had he used the signs correctly? But she wanted to learn Healing arts from Scree, and he wanted to spend time with his friend before she left.

Orm signed, "Did you get the chocolates?"

Drakor nodded. "They look very efficient. Thank you!" He gave his friend a bag. "For the marvelous meals you make."

Orm felt the lumpy bulbs. "Garlic! The flavor feels exquisite."

Drakor gave three small, clear quartz bottles to Scree. Each had a gemstone stopper: ruby red, sapphire blue, or emerald green. "To hold your healing potions."

Scree turned colors, matching each stopper. "These

are perfect!"

Taron grinned from where he stood near the mast, coiling a line. "It's good to have you back on board!"

"It isss great to be back!"

Karoon studied his friend. "You're even taller!"

Drakor smiled. "I have grown." He opened his wings and stretched, with a reach as wide as the skiff.

Karoon thumped him on his back. "Your wings are enormous! Arak says you might end up fighting Mardor again. You've both grown so he's still bigger. I can help."

Drakor automatically adjusted his stance as a sea swell rocked the skiff. He swiveled both ears toward Karoon. "How?"

"I was a dragonlet when my sire left for the star-fires. My dam lost interest in everything, even me, so I got into trouble. I got good at fighting and figured out ways to beat bigger dragons. Mardor will be ready for this fight, and I have some new ideas. I'll show you tonight."

Scree signed, "Remember, your plan matters more than your size."

Drakor snapped his tail in surprise and signed, "How did you know what we are talking about?"

Scree quivered with octopus laughter. "Dragons sometimes forget to sign while they're talking, so I learned to read dragon jaws. And it was a good guess, since you two *always* talk about fighting."

Scree tilted her head sideways, in a dragonly way, using a curled arm to support the weight. "You beat Mardor once. If you fight again, you can win again."

Drakor laughed. "I wish I was that sure I could win."

The skiff jerked against the restraining lines, as if eager to head back to sea. Water sloshed high in the tub, and Scree fastened another arm over the rim. "I led a battle against three enormous squid that attacked our pod. They were many times our size, yet we won."

Her skin cells changed colors faster than lightning as the fight played out across her body screen. Giant squid bashed their powerful arms into the sand. A battered octopus was flung far across the reef. Drakor's eyes were glued to the terrifying images. He had imagined this fight, but the grim reality was far worse.

"The next battle was inside me, so this fight was harder. I was furious. They killed my friends, a senseless loss. I wanted to give in to hatred, but I stopped myself. We marked the squid and released them, as planned."

Drakor nodded. "You let them go. That isss hard for an ice dragon to understand."

Scree smiled. "Squid are proud, like dragons. They hated that we let them go more than if we killed them."

Scree looked him in the eye. "Mardor has deep anger. This could flow into the fight, and into you. Drakor, what will you do when you win? Where will your anger go? What we do changes us and the world around us, like a wave. Anger and hate are dangerous waves that build on each other. They can damage you and the world around you."

Drakor shrugged his wings. "I do not know if I will win, how I will feel, or what I will do."

Scree twined arm-to-claw with her friend. She signed with two more arms, "You're a good leader. You can find a way to win both fights."

* * *

Dawn bloomed in cheerful colors that did not reflect Drakor's mood. After the feast, he went aboard the skiff and bid farewell to each of the travelers.

Last of all, Merika flew aboard. Her polished scales caught the sunrise colors, sparkling with a golden sheen. A shiver ran down his spine. Merika looked like she belonged with the golden dragons, following her dream. Would she even want to return?

Drakor bid farewell to Merika and flew ashore. He stood on the rocky beach, holding his hands up, claws back. Merika matched them from her place by the rail. The skiff grew smaller and smaller as the wind carried it away. Then all he saw was the sea.

Drakor folded his wings tight, resisting an urge to fly high and watch longer. He had a clan to manage. But a part of him left with Merika, and his snowy scales felt gray.

He turned away. "Jardor, could you take over here? I need to check on the dam again." Her egg seemed a bit small. Would the hatchling be healthy?

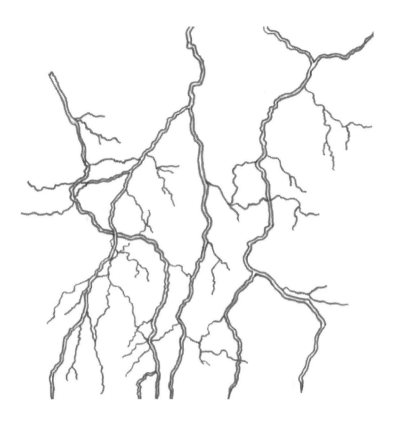

CHAPTER 12: RISING STORM

The rising wind blew cold and fierce. Dark clouds covered the dawn horizon. Then Drakor spied a lone white cloud. No, it moved too fast. He sharpened his gaze and his heart beat faster. A dragon was flying in from the south. Merika! He leapt into the sky and flew to meet her, landing lightly at the edge of the field.

Merika hit the ground hard, staggering as she found her footing. She wore her regular chest pouch and there was a new, bulky bag fastened between her wings.

Drakor flicked his tail in surprise as she stumbled. That backpack must be heavy! He sucked in his breath as her scales caught the light, sparkling like frost on new snow. Then he held out his hands, claws tilted back. "I missed you."

Merika met his hands, claws back. "I am just visiting."

Drakor nodded casually, hiding his disappointment. "Of course. The welcoming ceremony should start soon."

A smile lit her face. "Thanks for the trance-mind message. I hoped I would be on time. I flew morning 'til sunset for four days and camped on the beaches at night. Some of them glow!"

Drakor smiled back. "Trance-mind isss useful, especially over long distances." So far, only four ice dragons knew how to speak mind-to-mind. He had trained Jardor and Merika, and his sire learned from Arak. But if Mardor learned, he could plot in even greater secrecy.

Merika took a sweet-scented bag from her chest pouch. "Arak sent this for the welcome feast."

Drakor grinned. "Chocolate!"

An old dragon-lady landed beside him and bowed low. "It isss time to form the circles."

Merika flexed her wings excitedly. "The new dragonlet!"

Drakor snapped his tail. This would be the first ice dragon to hatch in the New World. He called out to Jardor, "The hatching isss now! Give the signal!"

BOOM! BOOM! Two thundering beats of the drum informed the clan. The sky filled with white wings like a winter storm, beating toward the nest.

Drakor joined the flurry of dragons.

Three fierce dragon-ladies made a triangle around the nest, guarding the egg. Volcano gems were tucked into spaces between the dark rocks: topaz-gold, sapphire-blue, and ruby-red. These gems caught the light, flickering like flames.

The dragon-dam stood with crisply folded wings, eyes glowing as she gazed down at her nest. Her egg was a precious jewel, smaller than normal but perfect. Thick, diamond-shaped scales swirled from top to bottom in a pine cone pattern. The dark bronze shell shimmered with iridescent, red-gold streaks, like a fire opal.

The dragons formed circles around the nest. Dragon-ladies made the inner rings, standing closer to the nest. Dragon-lords were in the outer circles. They all raised their claws to the sky and stood silent, waiting.

The egg rocked back and forth while the dragon-dam crooned encouragement. Pecking noises filled the waiting silence. Finally, the tip of a small nose showed through a tiny crack in the shell.

That was the signal.

Sparks crackled up from dragon claws as they called splinters of lightning. They added metals for color, matching the Volcano nest gems. Electric rings of red, yellow, and blue light surrounded the nest like an earth-bound aurora.

The dragon-inside pecked at its shell, but the crack did not grow. The pecking sounded weaker and weaker. Then it stopped.

A desperate silence filled the air, as brittle minutes ticked by.

Then Merika stopped her lightning display. She stepped up to the egg, reached her claws into the tiny crack, and gently pulled the shell apart. A small, damp dragon-lord fell out and lay limp on the nest grass, panting.

The circles of light stopped. Dragons stared.

A dragon-lord muttered, "He isss weak. We need strong dragons for a strong clan."

Mardor snapped his tail with a loud crack. "He isss a worthless runt. He should have died in the egg."

Another growled, "She helped him hatch! That isss not our way."

The new dam hung her head, and her wings drooped. "I am old to be with egg. My mate isss the only dragon who died flying here. Our new home has no hot sands to warm the nest, so I covered my egg with rotting plants. This warmed my dragonlet-within. And he hatched."

She gently stroked the ridge scales of her dragonlet and gazed into his clear gray eyes. "He isss my first dragonlet, my only dragonlet." Her voice dropped to a whisper. "But he isss weak. I should let him die."

Merika shook her head. "NO. He isss just small. Feed him fish eggs for extra energy. He could grow to be the biggest of us all!"

Mardor scowled. "The weak should die. It isss our way."

Merika threw Drakor a pleading look.

Drakor assumed his most leader-like pose and raised his wings for silence. "We welcome our newest clan member! Dragons are born of the Volcano." He looked from one dragon to the next, meeting their eyes with a confidant stare, forcing them to accept his decision. But inside, he felt as if he had wandered into thick mud that sucked him down.

This was the first dragonlet to hatch in the New World, and it was weak. This would be called Drakor's

Failure, a vindication for every dragon who protested their move here. By clan law the dragonlet should die, yet he had just welcomed him into the clan. Mardor must be thrilled.

A dragon muttered, "Will *all* the new dragons be weak?"

Shadows spread across the ground as the dark clouds grew. Drakor glanced at Mardor, who was already talking with the malcontents. His gut churned with worry. More than one storm was brewing.

Drakor raised his wings again. "Now we will fill the feasting table. Merika brought chocolate for the feast!" That got their attention as nothing else could. He headed for the table, bringing the restless crowd with him. Soon they were safely away from the new dragonlet, and Merika.

Drakor glanced back. Merika had helped the dragonlet despite their customs, despite the angry dragons. She had also helped with Drakor's crippled sire. He clicked his claws together. Why should the weak or sick be left to die? These dragons might heal and, if not, they still had much to offer. Strong was not everything.

Tempting aromas filled the sky as dragons brought food for the celebration. The new feasting table was beside their village. It was a long rectangle, about half as tall as an adult dragon, carved from a rare outcrop of solid garnet. The table was as important as the food that often hid its colorful surface. It was a symbol, a solid sign that this place was their new home.

The rock had all the garnet colors. Much of the table had blends of yellow, orange, and red garnet, like a flaming sunrise. Green patches sparkled brighter than emeralds, while a rare section had blue and purple garnet. Streaks of pink seemed to swirl in the light, like an aurora.

Most of the rock had been sanded smooth until it gleamed. Clusters of garnet crystals stuck out above the flat surface, like earthy red flowers growing from the table. This natural, untouched element was an important part of their art.

Dragons filled the table with long platters of fish. Dragon-sized bowls held festive salads made from sliced roots with nuts, seeds, mushrooms, and bright red berries. Other bowls had a colorful mix of lichens: golden-orange, silvery-gray, green, and bright crimson.

Drakor looked north, toward the rocky region. This was prime lichen territory, a perpetual source of this tough food. It should survive even the most brutal winter. Most lichens were safe to eat, nutritious, and tasted awful.

Drakor signaled his second-in-command to strike the drum.

BOOOM! BOOOM! BOOOM! Three beats rumbled through the air, announcing the feast.

Dragons swiftly lined up at the head of the table, on both sides, rustling their wings with excitement. As leader, Drakor went first, followed by his second-in-command. He clicked his claws on the polished rock and smiled. He chose their new village location partly for this garnet mass, to make a gemstone table that nearly matched the one on their island. This would connect their old and new homes each time the clan gathered to eat.

Jardor spoke up. "The table isss perfect, and the food isss even better."

Drakor gave a half smile. "At least *something* isss as

it should be."

Jardor thumped him on the back. "And we survived. That isss also good."

Drakor's smile grew. "Yes it isss." He added lichen salad to his plate, along with a helping of memories. For more than a year their island Volcano rumbled and stank, warning them to leave. Ocean fish heeded this warning and left. Ice dragons stayed but, without these fish, meals were lean. They scrounged for food, scraping lichens from rocks and branches. The clan remained on that island despite the warnings and their hunger, until he forced them to leave.

Drakor chose a thick slice of smoked fish, noting the pleasant woodsy aroma. He added nuts, seeds, and shredded roots to his lichen salad, hoping to improve the flavor. Then he sat with his three in-commands, who carefully talked about anything but the weak dragonlet.

Drakor chewed his lichen salad. The nuts and seeds barely improved the flavor. He drained an entire mug of tea, trying to wash away the lichen flavors of rotted wood and crumbling rock. Could spices from golden dragons improve the taste?

Mardor sat with the oldest, biggest dragons, talking loudly. "That new hatchling cannot even walk to the feast! Why did Drakor accept him into the clan? Does he *want* weak dragons? Clan members who can never challenge him? What kind of leader isss he?"

Drakor ground his teeth. He glanced back toward the nest. Merika and two dragon-dams remained with the new dragonlet, who was too weak for the traditional walk to the feast. They must all be hungry.

Jardor said, loudly, "The feasting table isss full."

Cranart added, "This fish isss delicious!"

Drakor nodded to his friends. "Thank you. Mardor isss right about one thing. The dragonlet cannot attend this feast, so his protectors will miss this meal. Jardor, could you take over here?"

Drakor slid the rest of his meal into his chest pouch; maybe he could slip away later and explore. Then he began filling three plates with food. While he was growing up, he saved part of every meal for his crippled sire. It became second nature to feed another dragon. Now he balanced three plates on his arms and walked slowly toward the nest.

Drakor paused not far from the nest, entranced by the peaceful scene. Dragons were sharing their precious journey food with each other and the dragonlet. They shredded the fish into tiny pieces and encouraged him to eat. Most hatchlings were ravenous, greedy, and self-focused. This hatchling ate as if he was too tired to feed, but understood their concerns and wanted to ease their worries.

Drakor gave his first true smile since the difficult hatching. This hatchling would be an interesting addition to the clan.

As he watched, the clouds above grew thicker, racing across the sky. Lightning sparkled and thunder rumbled. A flare of light caught Merika, and she seemed to glow a brighter shade of white.

Drakor's heart stopped. He stumbled and nearly dropped the plates.

The dragons turned as one, claws out, ready to fight anything to protect the hatchling.

Drakor cleared his throat. "I brought you food from

the feast." But, of course, that must be obvious.

Merika grabbed two of the plates before they could fall. She gave them to the dragon-dams, who accepted the food with wide eyes and quiet murmurs of thanks. One whispered, "No leader does this."

Drakor flinched. No leader had ever done this, and certainly not Mardor. It was an unheard of courtesy. He simply did not fit the leader role.

Merika took the third plate with a proper, formal bow and slid this food into her chest pouch.

Drakor eyed the empty plate. "You are not hungry? You flew far today."

Still not speaking, she shook her head no.

Drakor flicked his tail nervously. "Then, could we walk?"

She hesitated before nodding. They walked together in silence, to the open grassy field. Then she squared her wings and looked him in the eye. "What I did with the egg does not follow our rules, but I *had* to do it."

He grinned. "Of *course* you did! If you could not rescue a hatchling, then you would not be a Healer."

She frowned. "I thought you wanted to lecture me, to set me right."

"You *are* right. You are *perfect*. Will you fly with me?"

Understanding dawned in her eyes. She hesitated. "Are you sure? Mardor isss stirring up trouble. Another dragon-lady would be a better choice for you, as leader. What I just did will *not* help you."

Drakor looked back toward the feast. "Mardor will stir up trouble no matter what I do. This new dragonlet will be a good addition to the clan." He held his hands up, claws back, and she met them. Their hands fitted perfectly, just as they always had. "You are my choice, if I am yours."

Merika smiled and leapt off the ground.

Drakor followed and they spiraled up into the sky together, with perfectly matching wing strokes. His worries dropped away with the ground. Soon they were hidden within cold, gray clouds charged with energy. Lightning sparkled all around them. Ozone filled the air with its bright, bracing scent.

Light and shadow flitted across Merika. She caught a small lightning bolt and tossed it. He twirled the bolt on copper claws, making a bright circle. This was a skill learned from his games with golden dragons. He released it safely to the clouds and caught a new bolt.

They tossed lightning back and forth while Merika added spins and twirls. She must have practiced in the clouds with Dorali. She had learned more than Healing during her visit south!

Drakor felt that his scales must glow with the energy of this game. But it was no game. He took a bottle of cobalt powder from his pouch. This would make bright blue lightning, the sky color that meant freedom, the most precious gift. If Merika accepted this bolt and returned it to him, they were mated for life. They would share freedom together.

Drakor took a deep breath. He pulled the cork from the bottle. Then he caught a new lightning bolt and poured in the powder.

CHAPTER 13: THIN ICE

White lightning changed to the color of a bright blue sky. Drakor twirled the bolt while thoughts swirled through his mind. Merika was comfortable in her own scales, content with her life. When she left, he missed her calm wisdom and humor. But did she miss *him*? And, did she want a mate?

He took a deep breath and tossed the lightning.

Merika caught the blue bolt neatly and twirled it on her claws, as if considering.

Drakor's heart thudded painfully in his chest. *Why was she waiting?*

Then she tossed the bolt back.

Drakor's heart beat again with a normal rhythm. He caught the blue lightning, twirled it once, and set it free. They were mated.

Drakor and Merika flew up into the wind-stream, high above the sea of clouds. Clean, cold air rushed past, pelting them with grains of ice. They flew northwest with perfectly matching wing strokes, heading for the Volcano. Ice dragons were forged from fire and ice and so, by tradition, newly mated dragons flew through ice to fire.

As the sun set, evening colors shone up from below, washing through the clouds. The dragons flew above a misty, glowing carpet of rose and violet. Then sharp, bright stars lit the darkness. Drakor and Merika spiraled about each other, weaving a sparkling path through the night sky. They landed on a weathered plateau beside the mountain.

This Volcano was silent, with no vivid fires. The bright, living blood had hardened to rock, but the Volcano's gifts remained. Rare diamonds were made in its fiery depths, long ago. Now they would make new gems from the ashes.

The wind picked up, driving the clouds away. Drakor and Merika feasted beneath curtains of colored light that hung in the sky, rippling in an unknown breeze. They walked wing-to-wing across the wind-swept land, admiring its harsh beauty while gathering a few rare diamonds. Clear, eight-sided crystals had weathered out of the dark rock, sparkling in white, yellow, pink, and pale blue.

Drakor arranged the gems in a pattern that captured the flickering essence of northern lights.

Merika stepped closer and gazed down at the design. "That isss beautiful."

Drakor looked up at the sky with a sad smile. "Diamonds shine like stars and auroras, like the after-home of dragons. They always reminded me of my dam. The diamond she gave me was used in my hatching nest." He stood straighter and scooped up the crystals with his claws. Then he poured them into Merika's cupped hands. "Now, diamonds will remind me of you."

Merika carefully stowed the pale diamonds in her pouch. She reached a moon-white wing across Drakor's back and snuggled closer. "One day, these will decorate our dragonlet's nest. We would also need gems with bright Volcano colors."

Drakor grinned. "The storm isss rising. Feel the energy? We could make those gems now."

Merika tilted her head. "Why not?"

She leapt off the ground and climbed up into the air. They channeled the sky, striking the ground with lightning, melting hard gray ashes into clear gemstones.

Drakor gathered these new gems and presented them to his mate: ruby red, topaz gold, sapphire blue. "These stones have proper Volcano colors. They are of the Volcano."

Merika accepted his gift with the ritual words, "Dragons are hatched from the Volcano." She added them to her pouch and looked to the east. "Traditions are important. They keep memories alive. But this Volcano isss far from our home, and it isss late."

Drakor nodded. "We will spend the night in my ice cave." He launched into the sky, and she followed. Soon they rested together on a bed of dry leaves within sparkling, ice-blue walls.

Merika ran a claw along the cold, gleaming wall. "This isss the most beautiful den I have ever seen. But what will Jardor think when you do not return tonight?"

Drakor laughed. "Jardor will know why and take charge." He packed snow into their mugs and changed this to boiling water with a thin stream of dragon-fire. Then he gave both mugs to his mate. "Tea isss your specialty."

Merika filled two tea balls. "Red root, cinnamon bark, nutmeg seeds, and ginger root." She added her own special blend of herbs and put a tea ball in each mug. Fragrant steam filled the air as she added a pinch of pepper and a dollop of honey.

Drakor took a sip, then a long drink. "It isss perfect."

Merika grinned. "Dorali said you loved spiced red root tea. She gave me tea and spices from the south. I found local herbs that nearly match. Most spice plants need southern warmth, but I can grow ginger in my den. It isss useful for stomach problems." She sighed contentedly. "I have learned much from the Healers, but I still have much to learn."

Drakor gazed south, toward the land of the golden dragons, flicking his tail. "How long before you leave again?"

She followed his gaze. "I will help the new dragonlet for a five-day and then fly south."

Drakor wrapped a long, snowy wing around Merika and pulled her closer. "Then, we should enjoy this time."

* * *

Evening shadows stretched long as Drakor and Merika landed beside their village.

Jardor greeted them with a knowing smile. "It isss good to have you back."

Merika asked, "How isss the new dragonlet?"

Jardor's tail drooped. "Not well."

Merika sped to his den with Drakor close behind.

The dam bowed respectfully to Drakor and greeted Merika with an enthusiastic thump of her tail. "Thank you for coming! He will not eat."

The tiny dragonlet studied Merika with big, gray eyes as she crouched down beside him. She checked his eyes, pulse, and temperature. "He seems fine. What have you tried?"

The dam rattled off ten different foods.

Merika sighed. "One of those should have worked. We should try fish liver."

Drakor nodded. "That isss like chocolate to most dragons." He left to catch a fish.

Merika chopped the fresh liver into small pieces, noting the healthy maroon color and potent aroma. The dragonlet tried a tiny bite of the fatty feast. Then he turned his head away, rocking from side to side, moaning softly.

His dam's tail slumped to the ground. "Why does he not *eat*?"

Merika sighed. "This could be a problem with the food, his stomach, or both. We will figure it out." She fixed peppermint-ginger tea with honey. "This should soothe his belly."

Spicy-sweet steam filled the den as the youngster slowly sipped the tea. Soon he stopped rocking, closed his eyes, and snored.

While he slept, Merika cooked wild rice with finely

diced apples and herbs. "This should be easy on his stomach."

When the dragonlet woke, he ate only one spoonful of the stewed rice. He sipped the tea and slept again.

Following tradition, dragon-dams took turns visiting the hatchling and bringing tasty dishes for all. The den was drenched with tantalizing aromas from clan favorites, like the best feasting table ever. Each day, Merika tried new herbs and foods with her patient. He cried less but still just nibbled and slept. She sighed with frustration.

A visitor pointed to Merika's bag, which was leaning against the den wall. "What do you keep in there?" The silvery fish leather shimmered with rainbows, refracting light from the domed ceiling.

Merika opened her Healer bag and displayed the items in each compartment: herbs, vials of ground metal, bone needles, two types of thread, hemp bandages, poison for anesthesia, and sharp garnet knives in green, red, or orange.

The visitor stared. "Could I learn?"

Merika nodded. "Our clan needs more Healers."

Ten students attended her classes: dragon-dams, the youngster Jordana, and, to everyone's surprise, Drakor and Jardor.

The days grew swiftly colder. Summer was unnaturally short and, in less than a moon, autumn arrived. Wind rustled through the crisp, dry grasses. The storm-damaged trees were nearly bare, but any remaining leaves turned cheerful reds and gold. Then, within a dragon-week, the leaves were gone.

Drakor flicked his tail nervously as the days grew colder. He was not quite ready to teach the clan to breathe fire. He must solve the problem of Mardor and his surly followers before arming them with new weapons.

Each evening, Drakor walked with his mate across the field to the edge of the forest. The cold, gravelly ground crunched beneath his feet. The bare trees made lacy skeletons against a flame sky, like black coral in a sunset sea. Merika hunted for herbs while Drakor stood guard, searching for unnatural shadows. This was something that dwire could not hide . . . and their tracks in snow.

She dug up another golden root and added it to her bag. "Thanks for coming along, but the dwire still have not attacked. Maybe there isss no threat."

Drakor returned a half smile. "That would be comforting, if true. And maybe Mardor has no plans to fight me."

Merika snapped her tail. "But he lost! He cannot challenge again."

Drakor gave a mirthless laugh. "I do not think that would stop Mardor." He glanced back toward the village. "Will the dragonlet grow up like a normal dragon?"

Merika sighed. "Yes, if he starts *eating* like a normal dragon. I wish I knew exactly what to do. I spoke with Dorali and Zarina in trance-mind, and even they have run out of ideas."

A dragon-week later, morning frost sparkled across the ground--and the dragonlet finally began to eat! And eat. He devoured everything in sight.

His dam's eyes glowed.

Drakor sighed in relief. "This isss great! But why now?"

Merika studied her small patient. "I think he was just

too small when he hatched. He still had some growing to do before he could eat like other dragonlets, but the tea and special foods helped him along."

The dragon-dam bowed low to Merika. "It isss more than that. You saved my dragonlet twice, first from the shell, and then to live and grow like every other dragon. I owe you a debt I can never repay."

Merika gazed fondly at the sleeping youngster. "He isss precious. I helped because I could, so there isss no debt. Now I can leave and study with Healers."

The dam said firmly, "You already *are* a Healer."

Drakor grinned. "Yes she isss." He walked with Merika to her den and helped pack her journey food, secretly tucking in a precious bag of chocolate from his own stash.

Merika fastened her chest pouch. She slung the pack with her Healer bag over her back, between her wings, and tightened the straps. "You and the other trainees can look after the clan." As she turned to leave, a gust of cold wind whipped into her den.

Drakor stepped outside and studied the darkening sky. He furled his wings against the rising wind. "Wait for a better day."

Merika gazed at the swift clouds and her wings drooped. She nodded agreement. "But I must leave soon. Winter storms will be much worse."

Two days later, Drakor peered into Merika's den. "Ready?"

Her eyes glowed gold, reflecting the flaming sunrise. "Yes. Finally!"

A dragon-lady landed beside them in a cloud of dust. "My dam broke her leg. It isss bad."

Merika grabbed her Healer bag. She tossed in an extra roll of hemp bandages, handed two long, wooden supports to Drakor, and followed.

The elderly dragon lay sprawled across boulders at the base of a tall cliff, beside a thin waterfall. A broken bone stuck out through the torn, bleeding scales of one leg.

Drakor stared up the cliff. The smooth, water-sprayed rocks were covered with emerald-green moss. She must have slipped, but why did she fall so hard? And why was she up so early? The claws of one hand clutched a glowing mushroom, while earthy aromas escaped from bags beside her.

Merika poured tea and herbs into a mug. "This will help with the pain. What happened?"

"I was gathering, and slipped on the wet rocks. My wing caught in a bush, so I could not catch the wind to break my fall. Instead, I broke my leg." She laughed, but her eyes showed her pain.

Merika looked up at the treacherous cliff. "Why gather here?"

"It isss the perfect place: damp, with bushes, and the light isss right. I wanted to gather the glowing mushrooms, the type that stop bleeding, and it isss easier to find them in the dark. This isss also a great place for lichens. We should remember our old ways."

Merika smiled. "You should teach us, after you heal." Drakor pulled on the dam's leg while Merika guided the bones together. Then she wrapped the leg with a wooden support on either side. "This will hold it in place until we get you back home."

Six dragons arrived with a litter to carry the patient

back to her den. The patient's daughter walked alongside, carrying the sacks, with her eyes glued to her dam.

Merika flicked her tail nervously as she secretly signed to Drakor. "The broken bone tore through her scales. This isss a dangerous wound; she could lose her leg to infection." Her wings drooped. "I want to leave, but I should stay."

Drakor nodded. His inner jolt of joy was muffled by Merika's sadness.

* * *

A five-day later, Drakor set down a bucket of glittering shards. "I hope this helps."

Merika gave him a weary smile. "Thanks. Even with the herbs, oils, and micro-zaps, her leg isss still swollen to twice its normal size. It isss time to ice it again." She broke the shards into smaller pieces and filled two long bags. "The ice isss getting thicker."

Drakor clicked his claws together. "Yes, and there isss still much to finish before winter arrives."

Another dragon-week later, the morning sky changed. It was not shadow gray, eerie green, or flaming orange--it was completely white. This was a color all ice dragons understood: Snow.

White powder swirled around Drakor. The ground froze beneath his feet, and the snow began to stick.

Merika stared at the sky, and her tail drooped to the ground. "Winter came early. The patient's leg isss starting to heal, but I waited too long to leave."

Drakor shook his head. "You stayed for your patient, and you are learning new treatments every time you consult other Healers in trance-mind."

"But I cannot learn the micro-zap patterns in trance,

and that isss the magical healing energy."

Drakor wrapped his long wings around her in a comforting embrace. "Then we must find a way for you to return."

The snow fell faster now, sliding down his scales and gathering in drifts. All the smells were scrubbed from the sky, robbing him of the world of scents as well as sight. Drakor gazed in the direction of the dark forest. When this snowfall ended, he should be able to see the tracks of the invisible dwire.

*   *   *

Drakor opened one eye and peered up, checking the time. Sunrise streaks of red and peach glowed through his translucent ceiling. He took a long drink from the water-filled bucket, which was in a hole in the floor. Then he left.

The ground was white, and thick frost covered the branches like spring flowers. Winter was here to stay. But for how long? The stone walls were taller and thicker in these new dens. Would these changes be enough to keep the dragons warm during a long, harsh winter?

Drakor's breath made small clouds in the frozen air as he walked to the stream. Worn rocks near the edge were now covered with sparkling, spiky ice crystals. He broke through the solid surface and refilled his water bucket. The ice was definitely thicker, and soon this stream would freeze solid.

Drakor gazed south toward the silvery-blue shimmer. Collecting water in that lake was their next option. But that would be nearly impossible in a blizzard. And, eventually, dragons would need to smash through ice to reach the water.

Drakor clicked his claws together. Arak taught him to breathe fire. He could teach this skill to the clan, to melt ice. That would solve their water problem, but then he might face a group of fire-breathing malcontents led by Mardor. He was already skating on thin ice.

Drakor stared into the water-filled bucket, flicking his tail. Dorali, a golden dragon, taught him to use his inner energy to make the tiny lightning of micro-zaps. This was the magic of cloud sculptors and Healers. These tiny pulses of electricity could grow a dainty, fanciful snowflake or heal a shattered bone.

Each frequency had a different use and made a different ripple pattern in water. He just needed to discover a new micro-zap, a heat-zap, to melt snow into water. Heat-zaps would be safer than fire-breathing.

Drakor laughed. *Just* discover a new micro-zap. Then he straightened his wings. Well, why not? He would experiment at night.

Drakor swiveled his ears toward a crackling, crunching, tinkling sound. He leapt into the sky and flew south to the huge lake. Wind blew across the lake's frozen skin, breaking the ice into thin, clear pieces. These crystal shards piled up on the shore. Pushed by the wind, an unstoppable army of shattered glass marched inland.

Jardor landed beside him and stared at the marching ice. "I have never seen ice do this!"

Drakor clouted him on the back. "It isss good that we did not build near this lake. Nothing could stand in its path."

That night, Drakor experimented with micro-zaps, seeking a heat-zap. He zapped into a snow-filled bowl, using the energy pattern that weakened rock seams.

Nothing happened.

He tried two more zap patterns, to heal bruises and mend broken bones.

Nothing.

He added energy to increase the frequency. Surely *one* of his micro-zap patterns would work! But the snow remained a frozen, crystalline mass.

The next evening, Drakor tried a zap for sore muscles. He snapped his tail with excitement as the snow softened beneath his claws. He increased the frequency. The snow turned slushy and swiftly melted. His smile nearly split his face. Success!

Drakor put his claws into a bowl of water and zapped. Then he checked by candlelight, memorizing the unique ripple pattern of his new heat-zap. Now dragons could melt snow into water without fires or lightning swords. This would be a safer, easier skill.

Drakor threw festive sparks from his claws in silent celebration.

The following day, he summoned his in-commands and Merika. "This will be a long, snowy winter, so I found a new way to turn snow into water." He melted snow in a bowl, using just his claws.

The dragons stared. "How?"

"We channel *sky* energy to make lightning swords. We can channel our *inner* energy to make a heat-zap." He pointed to five bowls of water. "First, learn the pattern. Then teach the clan."

Three days later, morning light filtered through dense clouds. Dragons everywhere were melting snow with their claws. Some melted pictures in the ice, just for fun. Drakor grinned. Another problem solved!

Snow began to fall, covering jagged rocks with soft white curves. Then the wind changed, blowing faster and dangerously cold, like a frozen wind-stream. Drakor shivered as he tried to peer through the furious snowstorm.

Suddenly, the air crackled with energy. His inner eye caught a bright lightning strike, but he saw nothing through the thick white curtain. A soft boom filled the sky, muffled by the snowfall.

Thunder-snow? This was new, not even mentioned in their legends!

Drakor could barely feel the ground beneath his feet, and the tingling numbness warned of frostbite. He struggled home through the blizzard, finding his way with his inner eye: he followed a lodestone marker that glowed silvery-gray in his mind.

When these powerful snowstorms cloaked their world, even a dragon could get lost; they might freeze to death. So he created lodestone guides. Now, each den had a unique magnetic marker to guide the dragons safely home.

Drakor breathed a sigh of relief as he entered his den. Had all the dragons found their way back through this storm? His magnetic guides should solve *that* problem, but there was always one more problem.

Could he give the clan a reasonable explanation for the sudden, disturbing storm? Or would this new display of weird weather be another excuse to challenge him?

CHAPTER 14: LIGHTNING SWORDS

Two days later, Drakor stepped out into a silent white world. He walked alone through the slow white rain, nearly hidden within a snowfall that swallowed up sight, sound, and scent. Suddenly, a voice spoke up right behind him.

Drakor spun around, claws out.

Jardor jumped back and held his hands out, claws back, grinning. "Sorry."

Drakor thumped his friend on the back. "Are you really? What isss the problem?"

Jardor said, "The dragons are restless. We need something fun."

Drakor stretched his stiff wings. "It isss almost time for our Winter Festival. We will make new memories with our old traditions! Then the New World will feel more like home."

Jardor's eyes lit up. "That pebble beach isss perfect for lightning sword games, and we can play Slam on our small lake."

Drakor clouted Jardor on his back. "Tell the clan to prepare for the games. The lightning sculptors need to fetch the ice boulders. You and the other in-command dragons can take turns with the signal drum. That way, you can each join a game." His wings drooped. All but the leader could play.

Drakor straightened his wings. "Arak brought the rest of the lodestones, and I have chocolate for the feast. Look what I just found." He held up a heavy blue stone.

Jardor's eyes widened. "That isss a good omen."

Drakor nodded. "I hope so." Sodalite was a rare blue stone with white veins, greatly treasured by dragons. It matched the winter sky and their frozen lake, with its blue-gray ice and network of white cracks.

The domed roofs shed snow, but furry frost covered every den. This made small white hills that disappeared into the wintry world. Drakor paused to admire the peaceful scene, where everything meshed. He needed such unity for the clan. Then he sighed and brushed the frost off his roof.

That evening, Drakor placed the blue stone beneath his clear quartz shelf. He lay on his bed of leaves, watching stars through the roof, listening to the song of the lake. The ice crackled as it grew thicker, day by day. This eerie music was louder at night, when the temperature dropped faster. Drakor could tell how cold it was just by listening.

How cold would it get during this long winter?

* * *

Afternoon rays gilded the sea as Scree docked their small skiff at the raft. Orm tied it off, giving an extra tug to check the knots. They tossed all the bags onto the raft and then covered the skiff with a tarp.

Scree grabbed three bags. "I hope this keeps the skiff dry. That was a useful survey. The same types of migrating fish are disappearing from that reef, too. These fish must be leaving to breed or feed, but they're not coming back."

Orm grabbed the remaining bags. "I agree. It's not the chemicals *here* that are hurting these fish. Scree, it's good to be home. Our pod will love these treats: abalone, mussels, and that rare pink seaweed." He splashed into the sea.

Scree dove in beside him. She twined one arm with her mate and matched his spiraling descent. "Orm, we need to follow the currents farther to find the problem with the fish."

Orm sighed. "We also need to keep track of what's happening here. The threat from giant squid is real, and closer to home."

Scree nodded. "Scrim can keep watch here, and mind-call with any questions." She felt the flavors that seeped from their bags, sending a silent call to the pod. Soon, everyone would know they were back.

A blue-and-orange sea slug flew slowly by, flapping its clear, fleshy wings.

Orm stared beyond this creature, to the dark abyss.

"Scrim is clever. But *you're* the legend that the giant squid respect."

Scree flushed red. "I'm an octopus, not a legend. What we don't know can hurt us, and we know nothing about the fish problem. They're an important part of the reef, like notes in a song. If these notes disappear, the symphony of the reef could fall apart."

Orm twined another arm with his mate. "Alright. After the clan-and-pod festival, we'll follow the currents. But we need to plan carefully. If something is killing so many fish, this could be our most dangerous trip yet."

Scree's skin pulsed with happy colors. "Thank you."

Orm shuddered. "I'm not sure I deserve thanks for helping you into danger."

*   *   *

A five-day later, Drakor awoke as topaz and gold glowed through his domed ceiling. He poked his head out of the den. The skies were clear. It had stopped snowing! This was perfect festival weather. He left to find his second-in-command.

"Jardor, please announce the games."

Three strong drumbeats rumbled through the air. Dragons snapped their tails with excitement as they prepared for the games.

Cranart and Tenira glided over to join Drakor and Jardor. Choosing more than one official helper had raised many eye ridges, but things ran more smoothly. And why should the leader decide everything?

Drakor squinted into the rising sun as dragons skimmed overhead. They were all sizes, young to old, tearing joyfully across the sky. They landed in the middle of the small, frozen lake and immediately began clearing snow off the ice. They worked from the center to the shore, using powerful tail sweeps.

Drakor lifted a heavy sack from his pouch and gave it to Cranart, his third-in-command. "We could not have survived that long flight while carrying this extra weight. So, Arak brought our lodestones to the New World on his dragon-skiff. Use them to mark the ice for Slam."

Cranart rustled his wings anxiously. "And the game-stone?"

Drakor smiled as he lifted a lump from his pouch and unwrapped this. The top of the ancient, sparkling disc was covered with glittering blue sapphires. The gems were the color of the sky, of freedom. This powerful lodestone burned silver-bright in his mind. "I brought it from our island, since only the leader carries the game-stone. Soon we will play our first game of Slam in our new home!"

Cranart's eyes glowed. He bowed and left for the frozen lake, flying ever faster, as if the memories in these magnetic stones lightened his load.

Drakor gazed north, where huge ice boulders as big as Mardor stood on a field of snow. These ice blocks had been cut from the ancient glacier, floated down the river, and dragged ashore. A team of dragons pulled each block onto a platform of rolling pine logs.

As an ice block was rolled inland, a log from the back was moved to the front. Rolling logs traveled beneath each block to the field. Now, the field was ready for the contest for best lightning sculpture.

Drakor handed a sack to Tenira, his fourth-in-command. "This isss for the Lightning Sculptures. Make sure each pair of sculptors gets their share."

She peered into the sack and snapped her tail. "All of

the lodestones and black diamonds are here! I thought these were left behind."

Drakor smiled. "We brought everything we really need. Take turns helping with the games so you can enter them, too."

After she left, Drakor drummed his claws on his scales. Would these traditional games be enough to unite the dragons? Or was the clan too divided?

Drakor's ears swiveled toward a whistling sound. The young dragon-lady continued her simple tune as she strolled by him. This dragon lullaby held soothing memories of his dam crooning to him.

Drakor clicked his claws together. Music had an energy that reached into the mind, more powerful than a magnetic storm. He often played his wooden flute, quietly, alone. This was a farewell gift from Karoon, a golden dragon. Could music help bring the clan back together?

Drakor flew to the beach and signaled the drummer. A long, rumbling drum beat rang across the snow. Dragons landed in clusters and spread out, seeking the best spectator spots.

Drakor raised his wings high. "It isss time for the Lightning Sword games. The drum will beat ten times. The winner isss the dragon who hits the most targets before the last drum beat."

Pieces of wood were dropped randomly across the rocky beach. Then the first contestant stepped forward. He was young, barely able to fly, flexing his claws nervously. Then he stretched taller, held out his hands, and nodded.

BOOM . . . . . BOOM . . . . . BOOM . . . . . Ten slow

drum beats counted the time to strike targets with lightning. A gray haze and the scent of smoke blew across the field, but only three wood pieces burst into flames by the tenth beat.

Drakor nodded to the youngster with a reassuring smile. "You did well."

A dragonlet darted forward, slipping on the snow-covered pebbles. She grabbed the burnt remains, tossed them onto the frozen stream, and placed new branches on the beach.

The next contestant stepped forward, and drumbeats counted the time. When all the young dragons had competed, Drakor announced the winner. Then older contestants lined up, flexing their sharp copper claws eagerly, eyes bright with excitement.

Drakor flicked his claws out. A bright pearl appeared, glowing as he tossed it back and forth between hands. He could pull in more sky energy and let it grow, twisting into a bright lightning sword. He glanced at each target and found a magnetic wrinkle close enough to call lightning; he could strike every target. This was *his* game. His wings rustled eagerly, ready to fly toward the game.

Drakor sighed and released the bright pearl. He forced his errant wings back into stiff folds and watched with longing as each contestant played. He drummed his claws on his scales. Why did Mardor even want to be leader? Where was the joy in it? But power meant everything to that dragon, and he wanted it back. Mardor was a difficult leader on their isolated island. Here he might do anything, even attack the golden dragons. So he owed it to his friends to remain in charge for as long as he could.

Drakor announced the winners. The dragons left for the frozen lake, walking slowly so the dragonlets could keep up. Nobody wanted to miss the games of Slam! This brutal contest was their favorite.

Teams of two were roughly matched by size, with young, middle, or older dragons. There were pairs of dragon-lords, dragon-ladies, and mated dragons.

Cleared of snow, the frozen lake gleamed in the sunlight. Black lodestones marked the border of the Slam field, and were easily seen against the clear aqua ice. Drakor closed his eyes, testing the magnetic pull of the stones. He could feel/see each silvery shape. Players would know the borders of this game without looking. A plain blue stone marked each of the two goals.

Drakor ceremoniously placed the glittering blue game-stone in the center of the Slam field. Then he glided to a rise just beyond the lake. Dragons lined up along the icy shore, tails snapping, eyes glued to the game-stone.

Drakor raised his wings. "Each game of Slam will last for half a notch on the sun dial. Use only your tail to move the game-stone. Do not use wings or claws. No flying. No carrying. A point isss scored when a goal-stone is knocked out by the game-stone. The game begins at the beat of the drum."

Two teams of young dragon-lords took their places on the ice. Attackers walked to the center, facing the sparkling blue game-stone. A Defender stood in front of the plain blue goal-stone at each end.

The drum beat once.

Two dragons slammed into each other with a jarring thud, holding their wings safely back. They fought for the game-stone with whip-like strikes of their tails. One dragon curled his tail around the sparkling blue stone and slung it toward the opposite goal-stone.

Both dragons tore across the frozen lake, barely gripping this slippery surface. Sparkling shards of ice sprayed from their copper claws. They struck shoulder to shoulder, again and again, trying to catch the game-stone. The blue disc sped away and was claimed by another.

Drakor grinned. Slam was a good name. Tensions dissolved like salt in the sea as they played this rough, traditional game. The Defender stopped the game-stone, wrapped his tail around it, and slung it back. The disc twirled across the ice with a wicked spin. An Attacker caught the sparkling blue stone with his tail. Dragons crashed together as the piece of solid sky flew back and forth.

Finally, a loud crack split the air. The game-stone struck a goal-stone and knocked it out of the goal.

Jardor called, "Point!"

The players were battered, bruised, and grinning ferociously as they returned to their starting positions. Finally, the drum beat ended the game. Drakor announced the winning team while spectators thumped their tails.

More games were played with teams of the younger dragon-lords. The final winners were surrounded by exuberant friends pummeling their backs. "You won!"

The next games had teams of mated pairs. The game-stone flew across the ice while players gave impressive body slams. Dragon-lords had stronger tail strikes, but dragon-ladies had keen eyes and better control of the game stone.

The score was tied when the time drum sounded, so an extra time-part began, continuing the game. A dragon-lady slung in the winning goal with a perfect tail shot. The winning team flew triumphant spirals up into the air.

Next were Slam games with dragon-lady teams, then with the older dragon-lords.

No one was surprised when Mardor and his former in-command won, but Drakor was impressed by the violence of the final game. It seemed as if Mardor was pouring all of his anger into the contest. Would this drain away his frustrations? Or was the game just another practice for a fight?

The sun sank lower. Snow glowed gold in the slanting rays as Jardor beat the drum once more. Drakor announced, "The Slam games are now over. It isss time for the lightning sculptures!"

The clan hurried to the last contest.

Ten huge blocks of ice sat on the snow, glowing, waiting for the sculptors. A dragon pair flew to each block. They carefully placed pieces of magnetic lodestone into their ice block. These would call lightning, like magnetic wrinkles. It took great skill to place the stones in exactly the right place, imagining the sculpture within the boulder, knowing how and where to shatter the ice. Sculptors would use lightning swords of different sizes to carve their vision.

Drakor raised his wings for silence. "Dragons were created by the Volcano, from sky-fire and ice. These sculptures celebrate our story. At the first drum beat, sculptors will channel lightning. There will be ten slow beats. Stop at the last beat."

The ice sculptors raised their arms high, claws out.

Drakor signaled the drummer.

A loud drumbeat hung in the frozen air. Then the sky

sizzled and thunder boomed. Bolt after bolt of lightning struck each boulder, knocking off pieces of ice. The strong odor of burnt air mixed with scents of ancient ice.

Within minutes, rough dragon shapes filled the field.

Then the dragon-ladies deflected lightning with their claws, making bright splinters that ran down the ice, melting perfect wings. Next, they used splinters of lightning to melt the surface of the dragon's body. This liquid skin quickly re-froze with the crackled appearance of dragon scales. Black diamonds appeared like magic from their pouches, with the clear darkness of a night sky. They poked a large diamond into each slushy eye socket, which quickly froze to hold the sparkling gray Ice dragon eyes.

Dragons channeled the power of the sky as if they were true spirits of the Volcano. When the steam cleared, ten ice sculptures rested on the snow. Each was a perfect, larger-than-life dragon. One held a large fish in its teeth. Another had wings stretched wide in flight. A third dragon sculpture stood tall with sharp claws and snarling jaws, in a classic fighting stance.

Drakor shivered, recalling his terrible fight with Mardor. He checked each sculpture, noting the details and realism. These were true ice dragons, born of fire and ice, created in moments of magic.

Finally, Drakor declared a winner. The sculptors leapt into the sky together, twirling ever higher, sending lightning swords into the patchy clouds above. They spun a bright cocoon against the evening sky.

Dragons headed home, laughing as they hurried to the feast.

Drakor stood as still as the frozen statues. That victory

display was new, and his mind sparked with ideas. Ice dragons made only three lightning colors: white for games, black for warning, and blue for a mating proposal. If they used more colors, that glowing display could become sky art. And, if they added sparks, it would look even better. Green trees could turn to gold and then icy white, changing colors like the seasons. Lightning Pictures could become a new game!

Drakor's claws tingled with excitement. No, that was the cold. He blinked, noting the empty field. The sky had darkened into night, with starlight gleaming on the icy crust.

Drakor stretched his cramped wings and sped through the sky to join the feast.

*   *   *

Drakor woke early, in the darkness before dawn. He chewed a chunk of leftover fish and left his den, walking on a sea of blue-shadowed snow. The light of a million stars sparkled across the crystal crust.

Aromas from their dragon-sized meal still hung in the air. Dragons loved a feast, and chocolate made everyone smile. Even Mardor!

Drakor strolled to the meadow with a spring in his step, snapping his tail cheerfully. The winter games were a success. The weak dragonlet was gobbling food like a proper dragon. Dragons no longer muttered, "Let him die." Everything was working out.

He glanced back at his trail in the snow and grinned. dwire would also leave tracks, making them easy to spot. That was one less worry.

Then he spied part of a paw print. It was not his, and it was fresh!

Drakor froze. His eyes slid back and forth, seeking. But any trail had been brushed out. How clever! The dwire had used its tail to remove the snow prints and hide its tracks.

A cold beyond snow seeped into his body. There could be dwire right beside him, and he would not know! He scrutinized every hill and shadow, every lump of snow. There! That shape did not quite follow the normal curve of the land.

Drakor lunged forward and the snow leapt aside. Two more lumps slid closer. Then all three charged in to attack. There was no time to reach the safety of the sky.

Drakor gave the piercing warning whistle. He sucked in a lung full of air and bellowed, "DANGER!"

Drakor threw a lightning sword at the closest Dwire. It screamed, arched its back, and lay still. He struck another as it leapt straight at him. He channeled the sky faster than ever before. The third closed in and fastened its jaws on his leg. He twisted around and slashed its throat with one swipe of his claws.

More dwire appeared as if by magic. A whole pack raced toward him.

The dead beast still clung to his leg. He wrenched its jaws open, wincing at the pain, and flung the carcass away. He quickly felled two more dwire with lightning swords.

Then the pack closed in.

CHAPTER 15: CHANGING COLORS

The sky filled with wings. Bolt after bolt of lightning flew down from the hovering dragons. Snarling dwire screamed as they were struck by burning swords. Odors of sizzling sky and burnt meat filled the field.

The angry attackers leapt into the sky, trying to catch the winged fighters. Three more dwire attacked Drakor, the only dragon on the ground. He struck back with glowing swords that flew from both hands. The invaders lost their camouflage as they died, changing to a mottled gray-brown. They were about a third of Drakor's size, with sharp teeth, diamond-shaped scales, and no wings.

Camouflaged dwire fled back into the forest, leaving a clear trail in the snow. They wasted no time hiding their tracks. Then no dwire moved . . . at least, none that could be seen.

Ice dragons landed in a perfect circle around Drakor, standing wing to wing, waiting for instructions. He staggered to his feet and straightened his wings, ignoring the pain. He scanned the ring of dragons, noting who came when he called, and who did not.

Most were about his size, his age-mates, or a couple of years older. These were the dragons he played Slam with, the ones who challenged each other with spontaneous games of lightning sword. They accepted him as the leader in that game and now as leader of the clan.

There were three older dragon-dams. The rest of the dams were probably guarding the youngsters. But only two of the biggest, oldest dragon-lords answered his call. Drakor clenched his fists. Mardor and his followers had blatantly ignored his command.

Drakor relaxed his claws and stretched taller. He swiftly chose ten dragons who excelled at lightning swords, naming them as he pointed. "Cranart, take these dragons to hunt down the dwire that fled. Stay together and follow their tracks. Be careful."

He pointed to five more dragons. "Help Jardor drag the dwire carcasses beyond the field. We do not want to attract scavengers. The rest of you, follow Tenira and check out the village. Work in pairs."

Everyone left but Merika, and her eyes burned as she studied his wounds. "Sit down before you fall down."

Drakor folded to the ground. He gazed at the golden-orange streaks that glowed in the dawn sky. This contrasted oddly with the carnage below, where red patches stained the snow and gray carcasses lay in untidy clumps.

Merika pulled out a shiny silver flask. It turned orange, reflecting sunrise colors that were so bright, the metal seemed to be on fire! She warmed the flask with a heat-zap. "For energy. You need this."

Drakor sipped a sweet, spicy drink that warmed him all the way down. "Delicious tea. This has the perfect blend of cinnamon, honey, and herbs."

Merika gave a half-smile. "Energy should taste good." She unfastened the Healer bag from between her wings. Then she scooped up snow, washed the red ribbons off his cuts, and rubbed in a stinky yellow salve. "This has goldenseal, lavender, and yellow tansy to fight infection. These cuts are shallow, but a dwire's bite could be as poisonous as a snake's. Now, your leg."

Merika reached into her bag. She pulled out a sharp bone needle threaded with thin gut string. "This tear needs a few stitches. Hold still."

Drakor stifled a twitch as she poured stinging powder into the cut. Ice dragons did not show pain.

Merika held the edges together with one hand, carefully matching the scales. She sewed up the tear with her other, using five small stitches. "Scree does this so easily! It must be nice to have eight arms." She bound up his leg with hemp strips, testing to be sure the bandage was neither too tight nor too loose before tying knots.

Drakor held still, watching her closely. "Scree would be proud of you."

Merika beamed. "That isss the nicest thing you could say. And *you* threw lightning with both hands! That isss new."

He shrugged. "I have been practicing. We may all need this skill. The dwire planned this attack well, on a misty night just before sunrise."

She counted five drops from a vial and added them to the mug. "We are lucky you were here to give the warning. Drink this. It protects from some poisons. The wounds should heal clean, but be careful. I will check them tomorrow."

Drakor swallowed the bitter drink. "Thanks." He struggled to his feet. Then he pushed off with his good leg, beat up into the sky, and glided to the village. Merika followed. He made a rough landing, favoring his injured leg as he sank into the cushion of snow.

Zardan waved them over. "One got through. I killed it, but a dragonlet isss badly hurt." He gazed at Drakor's bandaged leg and raised one eye ridge but asked no questions.

Merika gasped. "Where, Zardan?"

He led them to the dragon's den, where a dam crooned anxiously to her youngster. There was room for only three dragons. Merika stepped inside. Drakor stretched his long neck through the entrance. His nostrils flared at the salty scent of blood.

The wounded dragonlet was swallowing screams, digging her claws into the ground, struggling to not show pain. One wing was perfect. The other was crumpled like a dead butterfly. Broken bones showed through the snow packed around her wing. Snow covered her chest, already stained red and pink like a terrifying sunset.

Drakor's heart thudded painfully, and his eyes blazed with anger. If she lived, would she ever be able to fly? Would she die, or wish she had?

His right wing twitched as he recalled that day, when the rumbling Volcano shook him off. That was the day that changed everything.

Drakor's wing was shattered. He tumbled down the mountain, rolled onto thin ice, and was carried out to sea. He should have died. Then he met the odd crew on a strange, floating home. Arak, Dorali, and Scree had helped. Now he needed them again.

Merika spoke to the dam in a low, soothing voice. "I can help."

The dam tore her gaze away from her wounded dragonlet. She scanned Merika's eyes as if searching for hope. Then she moved aside, making room for the Healer.

Merika knelt beside the youngster and stirred powders into a cup of water. "This tastes bitter, but it will help you." She signed to Drakor, *Call Dorali and Scree. We need them.*

He nodded. *I know.*

Drakor flew to his den to enter the trance-mind. He soon returned and signed, *Dorali will come. Arak will bring Scree.*

Drakor wrinkled his nose. Narrow wall slits were open in summer for air flow. The slits were closed for winter, making a snug home that trapped body heat. It also trapped the stench of bloody, fish-skin bandages and stinky herbs.

The dragon's chest was now clean and slathered with mustard-yellow salve. Several cuts had fish-skin bandages and three needed stitches, but one slice was so deep he could almost see her beating heart. This cut held golden honey, to protect the wound while it slowly healed from within.

Merika took out a fat roll of hemp bandage and eyed the wound.

Drakor saw the problem. "I can lift her while you wrap."

The dam scrunched back against the wall as he crawled in, barely fitting. Drakor gently lifted the dragonlet off her pallet while Merika wrapped bandages around her chest, adding pieces of iodine-rich seaweed to kill infection.

Merika motioned to the dam. "Could you collect more branches for her resting pallet?"

The dam nodded and slipped out of the den.

Drakor murmured, "It isss harder to see someone hurt than to be hurt."

Merika nodded. "She needs to help, so I gave her something to do." The dragonlet's breathing was slow and uneven as she dropped into a deep, herb-induced sleep.

Merika carefully brushed the snow off the wing. She finished just as the dam returned, with her arms piled high with branches. The dam trembled at the sight of her dragonlet's mangled wing. Merika gave her a large, carved rock bowl. "Could you fill this with clean snow from the top of the mountain?"

The dam rustled her wings nervously before flying away.

Drakor asked, "Why so far?"

Merika took out her needle. "It would be hard for her to watch this." She looked up at the cloudy, domed ceiling. "There isss just enough light for this work." She makes small, even stitches. "I used the thinnest gut thread. It should dissolve, which isss easier on the patient. If I need candles, I could light them by breathing fire."

Drakor shook his head. "We learned that from the golden dragons, but it isss too early to share this skill with the clan. Ice dragons are dangerous enough to each other without breathing fire. We can use strike-stones to light the candles."

Merika flicked her tail. "Wise decision." She stitched up another tear and dripped honey into a deeper cut. "Why did the dwire attack now?"

Drakor looked toward the feasting table, where scraps remained in the snow. "I think they were drawn by the feast."

Merika nodded. "Follow me." She crouched down and left through the entrance. Then she drew a wing in the snow. "I need a frame, the lightest, strongest one you can make, to hold her wing still until the other Healers arrive. I can start the healing, but I need their help."

Drakor touched foreheads with his mate. "You know more than you realize." He measured the drawing against his arm. Then he pushed off with his good leg only, pulling hard with his wings as he beat up into the sky.

Drakor returned just as Merika finished her last stitch. The frame was carved from a strange, pale wood. "This isss basswood, the lightest wood from around here. And it has no strange odor to disturb your patient."

Merika reached for the frame. "That was fast." She sniffed the frame and then hefted it, testing. "Light and odorless. Perfect! Why did you have this wood?"

Drakor looked toward the forest. "When my wing was mangled, Scree and Dorali used a frame to help heal

171

it. Taron taught me about trees, and now I collect wood. There were plenty of trees and branches lying around after that storm, so I built a simple den in the forest to properly store and dry different types of wood."

Merika nodded. "That was lucky. Why different types?"

"I want to make flutes and, some day, a dragon-skiff. I want to travel. Giant squid have a saying that isss both greeting and farewell: 'May you surf the tangled currents of the sea, forever.' The sea could carry us anywhere, if we had a skiff."

She stared. "You never mentioned this."

Drakor shrugged his wings. "Life has been busy. I add big branches to that den when I find them."

Merika ran a claw along the sturdy frame, feeling the rim and wing struts. "This isss well made. You make a good Healer."

Drakor smiled. "You say the nicest things."

Together they stretched the dragonlet's battered wing to fit the frame, gently, making sure the broken bones met properly. Drakor held the wing against the brace while Merika wrapped it in place using soft strips. She placed her claws on the dragonlet and ran them lightly across the chest, back and forth. Then she started on the wing. "This energy speeds healing."

Drakor stared. "I remember this pattern." He put the claws of both hands on his wound and began zapping. He could barely feel it. How fast did it work?

He learned the skill mere months ago, but it seemed like years. This was a simpler time, before he challenged Mardor in a fight to be leader. Now, he was healing a new wound while preparing to face an old enemy.

That jogged another memory from Dorali, telling him that the pulse could distract a dragon like unexpected storm energy. Micro-zaps did not break their fight rules, but it would feel like cheating. He used no zaps when he fought Mardor the first time and became leader. Only his fight strategy had been new and unexpected.

Drakor touched Merika's shoulder. "I will be back. You need to stay with your patient."

Jordana poked her head in, adding a breeze as she flexed her wings nervously. "If you need a helper, I can stay. I learned a few Healer skills from Dorali."

Merika smiled at the youngster. "I could use your help." She caught Drakor's eye as he turned to leave. "Your wing muscles are tense again. Drink some tea and relax. Be careful with that injury."

He nodded. As he left, Merika welcomed Jordana into the den.

Drakor walked away slowly, thinking. He ate a clawfull of nuts for energy. Then he stretched his arms and wings, loosening the muscles. Crisp, cold air numbed his wounds, which helped, but he would still need Orm's bitter candy.

Drakor popped three chocolates into his mouth and grimaced. How could chocolate taste bad? He pushed off with his good leg and flew to the field, where his second-in-command was finishing up. Dwire carcasses were neatly stacked just inside the forest.

"Jardor, please call my third- and fourth-in-command."

Two long whistles split the air.

Cranart and Tenira soared over and landed.

Cranart said, "We killed three more dwire. The rest

of them erased their tracks as they ran into the forest. Then they camouflaged and disappeared."

Drakor eyed the silent forest. "You did well. Call off your team. We will find another way to deal with them."

Tenira folded her wings crisply. "We killed two dwire in the village, and your sire killed the third one that sneaked through earlier. How isss the dragonlet?"

Drakor nodded. "Thank you. Merika isss still with the dragonlet. We splinted her broken wing, and two more Healers will arrive soon. Now there isss another matter I must deal with. Come with me."

They flew together to the meeting circle.

Drakor landed in the center. The icy crust crunched as it broke beneath his claws, and he sank into the snow.

Jardor landed on a rise just outside the circle, beside the huge drum. BOOOMMMM! The drumbeat thundered across the ice and through the sky. Dragons swiftly gathered, forming loose circles around the center.

Drakor took a deep, calming breath. Then another. He raised his wings high, and the dragons fell silent. "I gave the danger whistle and called a warning when the dwire attacked. That isss a call to defend our clan. Many answered. Some did not." He met the eyes of each insubordinate dragon, ending with Mardor. "Where were you?"

Mardor eyed Drakor's leg bandage, and the mustard-yellow smears across the cuts. He stared back insolently at the leader. "You are such a *clever* fighter, so good with lightning swords. We thought you could handle *all* the dwire. Surely you were just warning us to protect the juveniles?"

Drakor stared into his eyes. "That would have helped.

174

Where were you? You know the clan laws."

Mardor raised an eye ridge. "Laws? You have no problem changing our laws. We never *needed* that signal in our real home. The dwire are a danger because you brought us here!" His neck twisted as he turned his head in a circle, meeting the eyes of each dragon as if he was still their leader. "We left a good home. You led us from safety into danger. The dragonlet that was attacked may never fly. She may die or wish she had. It isss *your* fault. The clan deserves a stronger leader."

Drakor stretched taller and looked from dragon to dragon, reminding them who was their true leader while gauging loyalty by their eyes. Many could not meet his gaze.

The clan was divided. Mardor had spread his lies, convincing all he could that their old home was still there, that Drakor was unbalanced and power hungry. Mardor was fighting with hidden claws.

Drakor sighed. He was the leader. He had saved the clan, found them a new home, and fought off the dwire. Now he had muddy smears across his battle wounds while Mardor gleamed like new snow. Mardor *looked* like the leader the clan expected, huge and powerful, so it was easy to believe his lies.

Drakor straightened his wings into crisp folds. He spoke clearly, using all the storyteller tricks learned from his sire. "Our Volcano changed. It rumbled every day, and the ground swelled. The fish left. The legends warned us to leave. This isss the wisdom of our ancestors. Our Volcano exploded and sent a powerful storm across the sea to say farewell. The magnetic field shifted. Sunsets are like flames. These signs tell us what happened. You *know* our old home isss gone. We escaped just in time."

Drakor pointed to the ground. "We can know without seeing. Close your eyes. Feel the cold, wet snow beneath your feet. We know it isss snow without looking. We know our home isss gone without seeing the empty sea."

His voice grew stronger. "We were nearly starving. Now we can fill the feasting table. We will deal with the danger. We are dragons!"

Dragons thumped their tails, beating the snow flat with this sign of approval.

Mardor scowled. He raised his wings and began speaking without permission. "You offer more words but no proof that our home isss gone. You brought us to a dangerous land. A dragonlet was torn apart in the center of our village! The clan needs a strong, experienced leader to be safe here."

Tails stopped thumping. The watching eyes darted back and forth between their past and present leaders. Drakor met their eyes and his tail slumped to the ground. The clan was split in their loyalty, choosing sides like an octopus changing colors. Mardor was the long-time leader they feared but understood, enforcing a strict, orderly society. Drakor was the leader they barely knew who brought unexpected change and danger.

He felt as if a whirlpool was sucking him under. They escaped the Volcano. They could deal with the dwire. But the clan was not prepared for the greater danger: starvation.

According to legend, this winter would last through spring and beyond, maybe a year or more. There would be no fall harvest. They could still catch fish in the lake and hunt along the seashore. But the fish could leave. Sea life would move into deeper water, away from the frozen shore. Dragons needed to stockpile more food *now*, while they still could. The clan *must* unite behind him to survive the long winter.

Mardor scanned the crowd and gave a smug, triumphant grin. "I Challenge You." His words sliced like a sharp claw.

Dragons gasped as order fled away.

"Mardor lost! He cannot challenge again!"

"This isss not our way!"

Mardor snapped his wings wide. "This isss your sign for change. We left our home. We smoke fish instead of drying it. A weak dragon was helped from the shell. Much has changed."

A dragon-dam hissed, "Helping the hatchling was the right thing to do. We should not waste a precious egg. The new dragon isss now strong."

An old dragon-lord snapped his tail. "We need a strong leader."

A young dragon shouted, "We *have* a strong leader!"

More dragons joined the blizzard of opinions.

Thoughts flitted through Drakor's mind. They all mourned the loss of their homeland. But, many believed Mardor's lie that the island was still there. If he refused this fight, others would soon challenge him, since they thought his first win was an accident. But if he fought now, and won, his victory would not be a fluke. Everyone would accept him as leader.

Could he defeat this hulking dragon a second time? If he lost, the golden dragons would face a dangerous enemy. And ice dragons would starve during the long winter.

Drakor nodded slowly. "I accept your challenge."

CHAPTER 16: RIP TIDE

Scree's arms woke with a jolt. Two arms sprang back like snakes, ready to attack with their toxic tips. Another arm swiftly wrapped around the shaft of a spear. Then her main brain awoke, noting the pearly gray water of early dawn. Her eyes swiveled about, searching for the danger.

Orm was watching through the clear glass bars of her cave, and he was safely on the outside. "You're the most dangerous Healer I've ever met! I poked to wake you from your bad dream. I was worried."

Scree popped up and flowed over to the bars. "What was I dreaming?"

Orm shuddered. "Your dreaming-skin was blurry, not like the crisp pictures you choose to make. There were two waterfalls, one above the other. Two white dragons fought at the top. The bigger dragon won. He slipped down to the second waterfall and fought a golden dragon. Both dragons tumbled over the edge and crashed down into the mist. Then your skin turned dark, your arms curled up tight, and you were as still as death."

Scree flicked the tip of one arm up and down, up and down, like the tail of a worried dragon. "This was like being caught in a dangerous rip tide. I hope it was just a dream. Mardor could challenge Drakor and, if he wins, attack the golden dragons."

Orm nodded. "Arak knew there was a risk when he helped Drakor save the ice dragons, but it was the right thing to do. You must have dreamed this because you're worried."

Scree squished thin, squeezed between the bars, and twined arms with her mate. "I'll check the sea for messages and then visit the new Healing Station."

Orm nodded. "How's that working out?"

"Excellent. Fish and turtles line up to have parasites removed by specialists. Then octopus Healers take turns helping. With Strike's unique skills, we're doing a lot more."

Orm smiled. "That sounds efficient. The abalone and oyster farms are doing great! We have plenty of pearls for trade and extra food for our dragon friends. Stop by my cave at sunset, and I'll fix us a scallop-and-seaweed salad. I just finished my design on the back wall. This tapestry glows in *eight* colors!"

Scree turned happy-green. "I can't wait! I'll help feed

your artwork. Arak mind-called. More than half of the golden dragons have now moved to the New World. In a few more months they'll *all* be here! Then we'll celebrate with a clan-and-pod festival."

Orm covered his skin with pictures of feasting food. "I can hardly wait!"

Scree made a skiff picture on her mantle. "And then we'll follow the route of the disappearing fish."

Orm grimaced. "I hope it's not also the route of the disappearing octopi." He flowed away, carrying a large, lumpy sack.

Scree gazed after her mate. That sack must have the pearl seeds. Orm put the shell balls into live oysters and abalone. The animals covered these plain balls with many shimmering layers, turning them into lustrous pearls.

Orm fed special diets to the oysters, to grow different pearl colors: pink, peach, lilac, creamy-white, or black. Best of all were the abalone pearls. These blue-green pearls flashed with orange fire, like rare opals. Blue-ringed octopi found them irresistible, and happily traded their venom for pearls.

Scree ate a few clams and added their shells to her garden. Then she pulsed through the sea, feeling the currents, sensing. She waved an arm at the mottled brown grouper. He turned white, asking a question, and she signed back, "Not tonight." They often hunted together, when twilight shadows changed the reef. Then it became a different world. Life glowed, corals fought viciously for space, and strange new creatures emerged.

Scree dropped down to a sandy patch and held still, feeling the symphony of sound as it pulsed through her body. Reef fish spoke to each other with grunts as they hunted together. Crackle-pop noises came from glossy gray shrimp. The sharp snap of claws was surprisingly loud for such a small predator. This sound came from her new assistant, Strike, the mantis shrimp.

Scree glanced toward the Healing Station. She and Strike had combined talents to heal Tara, her long-time turtle friend. Scree removed the pulpy pink tumor from the flipper. Strike used his remarkable eyesight to find the cancer cells hidden beneath the tumor, and she burned them away with a targeted micro-zap.

Scree gazed east. The ice dragon island had disappeared, while the octopus volcano had now grown into a mountain. Both volcanoes gave strange chemicals to the sea, adding a smoky-oily flavor, and tumors were no longer rare.

The reef trapped distant sounds, so Scree twirled up to the rose-colored waves above. She pulsed in place, feeling the full ocean orchestra. Long, rolling beats came from a drum fish in the reef below. The patter of rain came from above. Waves crashed on a distant beach, and sand squeaked in the rolling surf. Then she felt an unnatural clang of two metal bars striking together.

Scree counted three strikes, pause, two strikes, pause, and then the signal repeated. Dragons were calling. Someone was hurt! She shuddered. What if her fight dream was really foresight?

Scree turned both eyes toward the unseen shore. She could light the signal fire on the raft above or talk with bar strikes, but this was crude communication. She needed to know what to bring.

Scree sank down into a tangled clump of leafy brown seaweed and camouflaged to match. She set her clever arm-brains on automatic, to remain as seaweed, waving above her hidden head. Then she plucked a shimmering pearl from one sucker, focused her main brain into the center, and entered the trance-mind. Her eyes glazed over, and her head fell back limp.

Scree's trance-mind flew to shore and overlapped with the waiting shimmer. Arak made mind-pictures with their sign language, which was beyond the skill of most dragons. Scree excelled at mind-pictures after years of making images on her body, concentrating to change the color of every cell in her skin.

Scree. We need your help

Arak. What happened

An ice dragonlet has a mangled wing. Merika has done all she can. Will you come

Yes. Meet me at the raft

Scree's body jerked awake as her mind returned. She peered through the curtain of leafy brown strands that swayed with the current. Then she relaxed her seaweed arms back into their normal octopus shape and pulsed home.

A mangled wing was bad, but this was not the terrible fight she feared. It would be great to see her friend Merika again. And Drakor! Yes, he tried to eat her when they first met, but once they resolved that problem, he made an interesting friend.

Red, green, and golden-brown strands swayed with the currents outside her cave. This elegant seaweed garden had grown, and soon it would hide the entrance to her home. Scree squeezed between the bars of her cave. She checked the spears that leaned against the inner wall. The sharp, poisonous tips were safely sunk into the smooth sand floor. These spears helped octopi defeat the attacking giant squid. But would that battle stay won?

The walls of her entrance chamber were now covered by Orm's living art, with a swirling mosaic that glowed in red, green, blue, and gold. Scree tossed a shrimp to the glowing jellyfish that lit a side room, which was used for patients. She flowed deeper into her cave and entered the largest chamber.

She looked up at the night sky. Orm had created this with glowing tunicate stars. Three glowing jellyfish pulsed near the ceiling, waving long arms that moved like an aurora. Scree checked her Healer supplies in this living light.

Long shelves wrapped around the room, with gemstone jars and seashell boxes that added all the colors of the reef. There were knives, needles, thread, supplements, seaweed medicine, land herbs, poisons, salves, sponges, and bandages. Three giant clam shells held live maggots to eat off dead skin, leeches to safely drain blood, and barnacles to repair a turtle's shell.

Scree ran her arms along the shelves, plucking up items for her Healer bag. The dragonlet was in bad shape, so she might need a bit of everything. She added a jar with thin sewing needles carved from black coral. Next was a spool of strong, thin, golden thread. It was nearly indestructible, spun from the roots of the pen shell. The roll of fine gut thread would be useful for making deep stitches that could later dissolve.

Bright pairs of purple, yellow, or red scallops made excellent hinged containers. These held seaweed, herbs, and supplements. Silvery shell boxes had dragon spices, used for meals and medicine: cinnamon bark, peppercorns, ginger root, and more. She added a red coral box with sharp, hollow needles from the fin spines of a dead lion-fish. The living fish could inject poison through these spines.

Scree chose an orange garnet bottle with a tight stopper. This held blue-ringed octopus venom, a deadly nerve poison from their small cousins. A tiny dose could sedate a patient, but too much would kill. She added a sleeping potion from murex snails, the type with the spiky shells.

Scree felt the unique, triangular sides of an amethyst jar with foxglove extract. This land-plant poison helped with hearts, so she added it to her bag. A wiggly cylinder jar was carved from a thick branch of precious white coral. This glossy container held slime, harvested from soft coral fronds that swayed with the sea. It was useful for fighting infection.

Scree added dead sponges, live leeches, and a surgeon's knife of sparkling green garnet. Next, a coral jar with salve made from the bitter eggs of a colorful sea slug. She paused at the rolls of kelp leaves, feeling the leathery seaweed to taste its freshness. But Merika, her ice dragon friend, would have plenty of bandages. Last, she chose lightweight journey food.

With her Healer bag stuffed full, Scree left her cave. She placed the clear glass bars back into their holes across the entrance.

Scree gazed west, feeling the pull of Orm's cave, and flushed gray. She would miss their evening together. His glowing undersea tapestries were a wonder, matched only by his company. She used stones to leave a quick message for her mate: a Healer triangle with an arrow pointing north. They would talk later in trance-mind.

Scree reached the huge rock anchors and pulsed up to the platform above. She climbed arm over arm onto the raft and glided across the smooth, damp logs. Then she examined the four small skiffs that were tied off, checking the knots. The rest of the pod skiffs were safely anchored in a cove along the shore.

Scree gazed up at the swift clouds, shivering as winter wind brushed across her skin. She often risked this dangerous journey to the surface just to admire the stars. Today she would fly with dragons, soaring above a sea of color-changing clouds. And tonight she would fly closer to those mysterious crystal stars.

A bright dot appeared on the horizon. This became three golden dragons. Soon, two males and a greatly scarred female circled above her raft: Arak, Karoon, and Dorali. Two dragons stayed aloft while Arak landed beside her on the raft.

Arak greeted Scree, touching foreheads in a dragon-to-dragon gesture.

Scree smiled, remembering the first time they met, when he crashed at sea. Now they shared a friendship as deep as dragon nest-mates.

Arak signed, "The dragonlet's badly wounded. Her wing's mangled, and dwire bites may be poisonous. Merika's still an apprentice Healer, and she's worried."

Scree looked north, toward the unseen patient. "Merika knows more than she realizes."

Arak gave Scree a small sack. "Yes, she does. Zarina sent this. You'll need the energy, since it's even colder up high."

Scree peered inside and her eyes lit up. "Chocolate!"

She popped a piece in her mouth and tucked the rest into her Healer bag. "Zarina's excellent cooking is exceeded only by her Healer skills. Thank her for me."

Arak laughed. "Now you sound like Orm." He unrolled a hooded cape.

Scree smiled. "He loves Zarina's treats." She studied the cape. She always wore a flying suit when traveling by dragon. The inner lining was woven from a soft, spongy plant to hold water and keep her skin damp. The outside had two layers of fish skins that enclosed blankets. The skins shed wind and rain, while the dry blankets within held warmth.

But this suit looked quite different.

Scree pointed to the rigid dome. "You've made changes."

Arak nodded. "I added eight thin, wood ribs to support your head, like the sea. This should make it easier for you to breathe and pump blood."

Scree beamed. "I'll finally know what it's like to have bones. And you changed the eye holes."

Arak clicked a copper claw against the clear, rectangular box in the hood. "I carved this from quartz crystal, to replace the open eye holes. Now your eyes will be properly protected while you study the stars."

Scree chuckled. He knew her so well.

Arak held up the cloak. "The inner blankets are thicker, for warmth. I added two slits for your arms so you can talk. The hood has side slits to add air to the water, for better breathing."

Scree eyed the new harness with its abundant straps. A cord wrapped around the base of Arak's right ear and ran to the harness. "That's new, too."

"This harness should keep you safe, even if it's a bumpy ride. Pull the line to my ear to get my attention. We'll fly along the coast so we can stop when you need a break in the sea."

Scree gazed steadily at her friend. "You've thought of everything."

Arak pointed north. "I hope so. This will be a much longer flight, so you need better protection. I made new octopus flying suits during our voyage across the sea." He dipped the cape into the sea and slipped it over Scree.

Scree squeezed her head up into the damp dome and looked out through the quartz box. "The eye box is perfect! It's crystal clear." She tied the cape just below her head. Then she climbed up Arak's golden scales, settled between his wings, and fastened the new safety straps.

Scree tied two ropes around her Healer bag and tested the knots. She fastened her suckers tight and signaled. The raft rocked wildly as Arak pushed off. Waves sloshed across the logs, gleaming bright in the morning light.

Then three golden dragons and one small octopus flew north to help a young, wounded ice dragon.

CHAPTER 17: THE CHALLENGE RING

Morning light glowed across the icy crust on the snow. White fog rose from the jaws of dragons as they stared, open-mouthed and wide-eyed. Then they backed away from Drakor and Mardor, clearing a larger space for the fight.

Dragon-lords marched in a line around the circle. Their feet struck the ground in perfect time, as if a drum was beating, or a heart. They stopped and turned to the center, spread their wings wide, and stood wingtip-to-wingtip. This living wall marked the edge of the challenge ring.

Drakor studied the fight arena with focused calm as he entered the first stage of trance-mind. Bitter herbs in the chocolate numbed his pain from the dwire's bite. He stretched, loosening his muscles for the fight. Dorali had said, "Size means nothing. You are as strong as your mind." But size did help.

Another ring of dragons formed close behind them, standing wingtip-to-wingtip in the exact center between two dragon-lords. Then dragon-ladies marched and made another circle. Dragon-dams formed the last ring, with the youngest members safely behind this final line of defense from the fighters.

The watching dragons stood perfectly still, as if carved from ice, with the electric calm before the storm.

Drakor and Mardor faced each other in the center of the ring, eyes glowing in the early light. They each took two long steps back.

Drakor's second-in-command stood on a rise just outside the dragon circles. He raised his wings high, and there was complete silence. "Fighting begins at the beat of the drum. Lightning strikes are forbidden. The victor will lead the clan." He bowed low to Drakor in a show of support, but there was a worry crease between his eye ridges.

Drakor crouched on the balls of his feet and dug his claws into the snow. His ears swiveled back to face the drum as he locked eyes with Mardor.

BROOOMMMM! The starting drumbeat rumbled across the frozen field.

Drakor and Mardor sprang forward with teeth bared, claws out, eyes battle-bright.

Mardor snapped his long, powerful tail around

Drakor's knees, like a whip.

Drakor leapt high to escape the living noose. His claws sliced across Mardor's tail as he whirled away, stopping well within the border of silent dragons.

Mardor crouched in the center of the ring as if he owned the fight. He ignored his cuts, with his eyes fixed on Drakor.

The leader feinted left, lunged right, and lashed out with the ten curved swords of his hands.

Mardor stood firm. Claws clashed together and sparks flew. The giant raked across Drakor's wounded leg with the razor-sharp claws of one foot.

Drakor glanced down at scarlet slashes that dripped onto red snow. His wounds must be deep, but he felt nothing.

Drakor began to spin, moving his feet in a perfect rhythm. He watched Mardor's eyes to anticipate blows. Soon he spun like a whirling tornado, moving in a circle around the challenger, darting in and out to attack. This was how Drakor fought and beat Mardor in the first challenge. He read Mardor's smile: this time, the giant was ready.

The challenger stayed in the center, turning to face the upstart leader.

Drakor whirled faster, moving his claws up and down in a blur to form a shield. He spun in and lashed out. Their copper claws met again and again, striking bright sparks.

Mardor wore an annoying, confident smile as he lashed out with claws and tail.

Drakor evaded the claws and sprang over the slashing tail, maintaining his balance. He shifted toward the east, still spinning, moving in a smaller circle around Mardor.

The challenger moved with him, pivoting to meet his claws, claiming the center of Drakor's circle.

Drakor leapt up and struck sideways with both feet, using the force of his entire body. He raked his claws across Mardor's thigh and landed back on the snow, still spinning.

Mardor growled at this surprise move as he struck back. He missed.

Drakor and Mardor fought in the middle of a crowd, but they faced each other in a private world. Their first fight had never ended, and now their claws were finally out.

Drakor moved farther east, spinning closer and closer to his foe.

Mardor struck lightning-fast with his longer arm. He broke through Drakor's defense, aiming a fierce blow to cripple the leader.

The crowd gasped. Fighters were expected to wound their opponent, but not kill, and crippling a dragon was even worse.

Drakor punched down hard on Mardor's wrist, stopping most of the force, but five new cuts bled down his thigh. His scales were sticky and his breathing was rough.

Mardor's smile grew into a wide, feral grin.

Drakor's nostrils flared at the scent of his own blood. He was covered in cuts, shivering as red warmth ran out of his icy-white body. He felt no fear, just a focused calm from entering the first stage of trance-mind. And he felt no pain, thanks to the bitter herb.

Drakor wobbled as he spun. He fought in a place

beyond fear and pain, but he was utterly exhausted from two fights. The fight would end soon, in victory or defeat. If he fell, Mardor would slice him to ribbons. This would be the most painful defeat the clan had ever known, and everything he had worked for would be lost.

Drakor reached deep inside, seeking his inner lightning. He had to win *now*, before he fell, to protect the golden dragons. He *owed* them. And his clan needed him, too.

Drakor stumbled and fell to one knee.

Mardor moved in for the kill.

Drakor rolled sideways and sliced Mardor's belly with razor-sharp claws, lightning fast. He kept rolling, jumped up, and dropped into a fighter's crouch.

Mardor's eyes blazed as he snaked forward.

Drakor flipped high above his opponent, sailing through the sky, as if he had just begun to fight. He raked Mardor on the neck as he spun overhead, using both hands, claws out, slashing an "X". This was the traditional mark of a defeated dragon.

Drakor had not marked Mardor when he beat him the first time, winning the challenge fight on their island. He hoped to lead without this custom. But the giant had never acknowledged his own defeat or accepted Drakor as the new leader. Marking him now was a move intended to rattle this cool, composed, deadly foe.

It worked.

Mardor roared in anger.

Drakor leapt back, to the east, ready for a mad, careless attack.

But instead, enraged beyond reason, Mardor threw a lightning sword straight at Drakor's heart.

Drakor deflected the bolt, sending it into the sky, seeking the safest path to protect the crowd.

Dragons gasped in disbelief. Mardor had just broken their oldest rule!

Drakor stared. This was a fight to the death with no rules and everyone at risk. He must end it now, before someone was killed.

Beating Mardor was difficult. Killing him would be easy.

Drakor instinctively gathered sky energy. He had the lightning sword skills to get through Mardor's defenses. He could throw a sword into Mardor's heart and stop him now. The clan would be safe. He would be safe. No one would blame him, and his biggest problem would be solved. But how would it feel, to kill a dragon? How would it change him to kill one of his own?

Drakor deflected another lightning sword, sending it beyond the rings of dragons. He must act now. But he just could *not* send that fatal sword. He let his energy pearl bleed away into the sky as he charged his challenger.

Drakor leapt into the air, striking Mardor square in the chest with both feet.

Mardor staggered back, off balance. His left leg dropped down into a snow-covered hole.

Drakor leapt sideways and struck Mardor in the belly, slicing with his claws as he spun away.

The giant toppled back and hit the ground hard, with his leg still in the hole. There was a sharp, crunching sound. Mardor winced but made no noise, even though his leg must have broken.

Drakor grabbed Mardor by the throat, forcing his own angry claws back. He needed to win, not kill.

"YIELD."

Mardor pressed an arm tight against his own bleeding belly. His eyes blazed, angry and defiant but no longer insane. He twisted and kicked out with his good leg, hard, one last time.

Drakor felt a thump but no pain as he stared into Mardor's eyes. His foe grinned and passed out.

Drakor struggled to his feet. He raised his wings high in victory, still in battle heat and feeling no pain. Even Mardor's followers could not question this win. "I AM YOUR LEADER!"

Drakor turned slowly in a circle.

The crowd bowed as one, but their eyes bulged and their mouths hung open. Every dragon was staring at his chest.

Drakor glanced down. His scales were sunset red. Blood spurted from the long, gaping slashes, and his bones showed through. This was a mortal wound.

Drakor whispered, "He got me." Then he collapsed onto the scarlet snow as his mind drifted away.

CHAPTER 18: SPIRIT DRAGON

Merika screamed, "NO!" She tore through the rings of dragons and fell to her knees beside Drakor. Blood ran from the long, deep cuts that sliced across his chest and belly. Was he even breathing?

The clan stared at the fallen dragons, eyes wide, flicking their tails nervously. Being torn between two leaders was terrible. This was worse. One was dead or dying, the other defeated and disgraced.

Merika trembled as thin white fog rose from Drakor's

jaws. Was his spirit dragon leaving? Then his chest moved, just barely.

Merika grabbed clumps of dried peat moss from her Healer's bag and pushed this into the worst wounds. She laid her forearm along the moss and applied pressure. "Moss will absorb blood, stop the bleeding, and prevent infections," she said, reciting a lesson. Then she wrapped long strips of hemp around the moss-covered wounds and tied them snugly.

Merika scooped snow from a rare clean patch, filled fish-skin bags, and pressed them onto the bandages. "Cold helps stop the bleeding." Reciting the lessons was oddly comforting, as if other Healers shared her burden.

Whispers flew around the rings. "Who will lead?"

Jardor joined Merika in the center and tilted his head in silent question.

She stared at her fallen mate and whispered, "He isss more dead than alive. I will do all I can. Arak, Scree, and two others are already on their way here to help the wounded dragonlet. They might heal Drakor . . ." Her voice caught in her throat, ". . . if he lives that long. He needs to be taken to his den."

Jardor glanced at Mardor. The giant lay where he fell, silent and still, with one leg bent at an odd angle.

Jardor pointed to two dragons. "Bring both toboggans, quickly."

Minutes later, five dragons lifted Drakor onto a long, wooden toboggan. Jardor said, "Pull him into his den, gently."

Merika gazed at her fallen mate. "Tenira and Cranart, please keep pressure on his wounds. Cover him with blankets when you reach his den."

Two dragons pulled Drakor across the snow along the smoothest path. Cranart and Tenira walked by his side, pressing against his bandaged wounds.

Merika tore her eyes away from Drakor and turned to the fallen giant. She knelt down beside Mardor and cleaned his cuts with snow, then used the stinging, mustard-yellow salve. He remained as still as ice, with vacant eyes, as if he felt nothing at all. She made a wide, hasty bandage around the worst wound, wrapped his leg straighter, and called Jardor. "Please take Mardor to his den. I will set his leg later."

Jardor eyed the giant. "I hope this toboggan can carry him." He summoned three large, sturdy dragons. "Pull Mardor into his den and then remain outside. He must not leave."

Merika said to Mardor, "Do not try to stand. I will check on you soon."

The giant slid his body sideways, up onto the toboggan, but his feet and long tail hung off the end. The guards strained against the ropes, grunting as they pulled the immense load. Mardor's clawed feet left a red trail in the snow.

Merika shivered. This trail had the blood of two dragons.

The clan stared after Mardor, snapping their tails.

"Mardor broke the law. He must die!"

"Kill him!"

Jardor raised his wings for silence. "I am second-in-command. I am the leader until Drakor isss well. We will wait for his decision on Mardor. Now there isss work to do."

Merika bowed to Jardor, launched into the sky, and

flew like the wind to her mate. Drakor lay inside his cave, as still as death. She quickly checked the patient. His pupils were huge, his scales were cool, and his pulse was racing. "He isss in shock. I need more blankets to keep him warm."

Merika whispered, "Do not die." She sent the gentlest micro-zap into Drakor's heart, to encourage it to keep beating.

Two dragons arrived within minutes, bearing tall stacks of blankets. Merika tucked layers of blankets around Drakor. "Raise the legs higher than the heart," she murmured, again reciting lessons. She folded two more blankets and placed them beneath his legs.

Merika cleaned his many cuts with snow and slathered mustard-yellow salve across them. She sewed up three deeper cuts using small, even stitches while carefully matching the scales on either side. Then she filled the deepest cuts with honey, to let his body heal them from the inside out.

Merika took a long, deep breath. It was time to check the terrible slashes across Drakor's chest and belly. She untied the bandage and sighed. She had stopped the bleeding from these death slices, but now his scales had an unhealthy, gray-blue tinge.

How did you balance the opposite needs of the body? When was a bandage tight enough to control bleeding, yet loose enough to allow the circulation his body needed? She gently cleaned the cuts and nervously adjusted the bandages. Was this right?

Merika turned to her helper. "Watch him carefully. Drakor must not move. I will be back soon." Tail dragging, she left for Mardor's den. She flexed her claws in frustration, wanting to shred something. Why did they need to fight *today*?

Mardor sat on his bed of leaves, staring at the ground. He barely looked up as Merika entered. His face held a lost look, and his wings drooped in defeat.

Merika's anger faded away. Scree's words came to mind: *What will be, will be. And then I'll fix it.* Well, there was plenty to fix. When would the Healers arrive?

Merika cleaned Mardor's wounds with clawfulls of snow. "The cold will reduce swelling." She slathered on the mustard-yellow salve, wrapped deeper cuts with bandages, and eyed the long belly slash. "This needs stitches."

Merika threaded a sharp bone needle with thin fish gut. "Hold still while I sew up your wound." Mardor sat as if carved from ice while she worked.

With the help of a guard she set Mardor's broken leg, pulling until the bone snapped back into place. He barely winced. She placed a flat stick on either side, wrapped the leg tightly with hemp bandages, and made strong knots.

Merika took deep, slow breaths while the image of a micro-zap pattern formed in her mind. She zapped through the bandages. This complicated energy pattern would help the bones heal faster. She crushed a clawfull of herbs, adding a pleasant, earthy aroma to the den, and mixed them into his mug of water. "Drink. This has nettles and boneset herb, to help heal your bones and scales."

Mardor did not move, so she put the mug into his clawed hands. "Drink."

He drank the potion automatically, without a shred of notice.

Merika collected the empty mug. "Mardor, DO NOT put any weight on this leg. A dragon will bring you crutches to help you move. I will check on you tomorrow."

He did not reply.

Merika crouched down to catch his eye. "Do you understand?"

Mardor nodded once and then continued to stare into space, as if lost in his own private nightmare.

The sun sank behind the purple mountain as Merika trudged back toward Drakor's den. The sky turned a vivid blend of ruby, gold, and topaz fire. She stopped and stared. How could such beauty exist beside these terrible wounds?

Merika entered the den and paused, overwhelmed by the stench. She replaced a blood-soaked bandage while Drakor lay still, barely breathing, dead to the world. Would he ever wake?

Merika checked the wooden tub. It was still empty. She called Jardor and pointed, "This must be filled with seawater before Scree arrives. Could dragons fly to the shore and bring back buckets of the sea?"

Suddenly, she swayed and nearly fell.

Jardor grabbed Merika's arm to steady her. He studied her eyes. "I will assign dragons to prepare for our guests. *You* need to eat. You have been working since the dwire attacked at dawn." He motioned to the other dragon. "Feed her and make sure she rests." Then he left.

* * *

Merika awoke at dawn, disoriented. She had crashed into sleep while lying on a few extra blankets. She sat up and turned to her mate. Drakor was completely still, lost to the world. She checked his pulse and put an ear to his chest. Weak pulse, rapid heartbeat, shallow breathing. He was still in shock.

Merika flicked her tail nervously and murmured, "If he does not wake soon. . ." She could not finish that thought. She gazed south, willing the visitors to fly faster. Scree and Dorali had healed Drakor once before. Could he survive until they arrived?

During the night, Zardan had taken the place of the helper. He stared down at his son and shivered with a cold beyond winter. "My mate sang him the same lullaby each night. Maybe it will reach him." He began to croon softly.

If Drakor heard, he gave no sign.

Merika flinched at the stench as she removed old, blood-soaked bandages. She rubbed lavender oil across his wounds and placed a gray leech on a dangerously swollen lump. It quickly attached, gently thinning and sucking out the old, dark blood to let new blood circulate. She wrapped clean bandages around her mate and tied the ends.

Merika chewed a handful of nuts for energy while rummaging through her Healer bag. She chose three small bottles and massaged the oils into his chest. "Hawthorn, ginger, and rosemary. This will reduce swelling and strengthen the heartbeat." Saying it out loud seemed to make it real.

Merika inhaled the spicy-earthy combination of oils and noted a salty smell. She checked the tub. It was full of seawater! She must have slept deep to hear nothing, while dragons filled the tub. "Now, what was that other heart oil? The dangerous flower?" She found the odd, triangular, amethyst jar. "Foxglove!"

Merika poured five drops on Drakor's chest. She rubbed them in and gently zapped a heart healing pattern. Nothing changed. "At least you are still alive," she whispered.

*　　*　　*

On the morning of the third day, three bright stars appeared on the horizon. Arak, Dorali, and Karoon glowed gold in the early light. They landed beside a waiting dragon.

Jardor stood in the snow, holding a tray with three large, steaming mugs and one small cup. He gave a wide, toothy smile as they approached. "You must be cold. Thank you for coming! Did Merika give you the latest news?"

Arak nodded. "Yes." He gulped his tea, noting the spices and honey. It was red root tea, the traditional drink of golden dragons. Jardor's thoughtfulness warmed him as much as the tea. "Thank you. We'd like to see Drakor now."

Jardor bowed low. "Follow me."

They all jogged to Drakor's den, which was near the edge of the village. Ice dragons turned to stare with wide eyes.

When they reached the den, Karoon spread a wing possessively over Dorali.

She curved her neck around to peer into his eyes and then glanced down at his wing. "Why?"

Karoon flicked his tail nervously. "I thought you'd just be helping a dragonlet. Now you'll be spending time with Drakor, too."

Dorali smiled. "Drakor's a good friend and a well-made dragon. But he has Merika. And I have you."

A huge grin spread across Karoon's face. "Yes you do."

Light gleamed off Dorali's sparkly green arm band. Arak grinned. Karoon had given that to her. Was she finally ready to accept him as mate?

A young dragon-lord stood at the den entrance, flicking his short tail nervously. He stood straighter as they appeared and gave the visitors a proper bow, bending at the waist with his back straight. "It isss my turn to carry messages. Are you here to help?"

Arak nodded. "Yes. Here are two more Healers: Scree and Dorali."

Relief showed in the youngster's eyes. "Thank you for coming so far to help our leader.

Arak crouched low and crawled through the narrow entrance tunnel, still carrying Scree between his wings. As his head cleared the tunnel, he stopped cold. Merika had shared her shocking news in trance-mind. But the reality was far worse.

Drakor looked like a corpse.

Flickering candles added light and shadows to the disturbing scene within. Drakor lay as still as death, swathed in blankets, with dull scales and a sunken-in face. Merika's wings hung limp. She sat beside her mate, gently stroking her hands down his neck, along the veins beneath his scales. She must be trying to send blood back to his heart.

Arak's tail slumped to the ground. Merika must be living in a nightmare. He and his friends left home before the challenge fight, before two more dragons were wounded. Had they brought the supplies they needed for Drakor? Could Scree heal his dying friend?

CHAPTER 19: HIDDEN CLAWS

Arak's nostrils flared as he entered the den. There was fresh sand on the floor and a minty scent in the air, but the smell of dragon blood lingered.

Merika's eyes lit up. "Arak! Scree!" She pointed to the wood basin beside Drakor. "Jardor filled it with water from the sea, and I have kept it warm with heat-zaps."

Scree slipped out of the thick cape, climbed off Arak's back, and slid into the welcoming warmth. She slowly curled and uncurled each of her arms. Her pale gray skin regained its normal red-brown color as she rested in her element, taking deep pulses of oxygen-water. "That was an interesting sky journey. Winter clouds are even colder than the deep abyss. I was half-frozen."

Arak quietly signed to Scree, "Please heal our friend." He turned to Merika. "I'll wait outside so there's room for Dorali."

*   *   *

Scree slipped two arms out of the tub, tasting the damp air in Drakor's den. Scents of old blood, potions, and salves were nearly masked by the potent aroma of crushed peppermint leaves. Despite her obvious exhaustion, Merika had remembered the importance of scent. Her ice dragon friend was already a true Healer.

Scree signed, "I'm ready."

Merika pulled back the blankets that covered the patient's chest.

Scree moved three arms over Drakor, sensing. Her skin flushed dark gray with worry. How was he still alive? He was cold despite the many blankets that were still tucked around his sides and over his legs and arms. Dragons needed regular meals. It was nearly impossible to feed an unconscious patient, so he must have eaten nothing for three days. His body salts tasted off. But worst of all, Drakor's heart fluttered erratically, and his pulse was so weak she could barely feel it.

Scree turned topaz brown with resolve. She was a Healer. Her arms sparkled with ideas as her main brain considered the options.

Scree reached into her Healer bag, grabbed the amethyst jar with the triangle sides, and pulled out the stopper. Her arms curled away at the sharp feel/taste. This medicine came from a deadly purple flower, and too much could kill.

Merika nodded. "Foxglove. I used that, but just a little. I was afraid to use too much."

Scree mixed ten drops of Foxglove extract into a spoonful of nut oil. "You did well. You kept him alive. Now his heart needs a stronger beat before I reset the rhythm. Drip this under his tongue, slowly, near the back."

Scree placed her arms above Drakor's heart while Merika treated the patient. Her sensitive suckers checked his chemicals, temperature, and pulse. She smiled as his pulse improved.

Scree fastened one arm directly above each of his four heart chambers. Then she zapped once into each chamber, in a rapid sequence.

Nothing changed.

Scree sent stronger pulses of electric energy into Drakor, again in the proper sequence for a dragon's beating heart. And then again.

Suddenly, Drakor coughed. His eyelids fluttered like the wings of a dying moth. A crack opened up, as if he was peering in from beyond. Then he opened his eyes for the first time since the fight.

Merika snapped her tail. "Drakor!"

Dorali cheered while Scree turned bright emerald shades of happy-green.

Drakor gazed at his mate and tried to sit up. "Meh-ri-kah," he croaked.

She put both hands on his chest, gently. "Do NOT move. Your wounds are too deep. You must lie still."

She turned to Scree and bowed low. "You saved him.

That was an amazing treatment only an octopus could manage. Sometimes I think I would trade my wings for eight marvelous octopus arms."

Scree grinned. "And I might trade my arms for dragon wings, to fly through auroras and up to the stars."

Merika bowed again. "Scree, I will fly you wherever you wish to go, whenever you want to go." She turned to Drakor, and her stormy gray eyes flashed with anger. "WHY??? Why did you need to fight NOW? I already had one horribly wounded dragon to heal! Then I had three! I worked every day, all day, on wounded dragons. I did nothing else until Scree and Dorali arrived."

Drakor watched warily from his bed.

Merika snapped her tail angrily. "When I heard the drum, I left the dragonlet with her dam and Jordana. There you were, locked in a terrible fight with Mardor. It looked like a fight to the death, and it nearly was. You *already* had a *leg wound*! I did *not* become a Healer just to keep fixing you up!"

Drakor attempted a smile and croaked out, "But it isss a nice benefit from having you for my mate."

Merika glared back and he cringed. If eyes could throw lightning swords, he would be dead.

"I *warned* you to be careful. You could *at least* have waited. *Why* did you accept Mardor's challenge?"

Drakor reached out one hand, hesitantly, claws back.

Merika stared silently, ignoring his appeal. Then she sat down beside him and met his hand, claws back. "I thought you would die, and you nearly did. I need to know *why*."

Drakor tried to nod, and winced with pain. "Merika, the clan was divided. Many did not accept me as leader.

And many ignored my call to defend the clan."

He took a few deep, slow breaths. "Half the dragons believed Mardor's lies. When he challenged me, I had a choice. I could fight Mardor now, when I had a plan, or wait to be challenged by other dragons. If I beat him, I would be accepted as leader. Few would want to challenge a dragon who could beat Mardor twice! I need the support of the entire clan for us to survive this winter, and the dwire. There isss much work to do."

Merika sighed. "At least you had a plan. But plans seldom work as expected."

Drakor started a laugh that became a dry, choking cough.

She held a flask to his mouth. "Water. Take small sips."

He drank the entire flask, slowly. "Thanks. I cannot remember ever being so thirsty! Yes, plans are not perfect. But dragon-lords may be less eager to challenge me after this terrible fight. I want to change how we choose our leaders. Our way isss a waste of dragons. Golden dragons have a sensible way."

Merika bent down and gently touched foreheads with her mate. "At least we can agree on that." She took another flask from her bag. "Drink this broth. I added the salts you need and some pain medicine. It isss not good to hurt so much."

Jardor poked his head in through the entrance and entered the den, smiling. "Drakor, it isss so good to see you awake! Merika and Dorali, the dragonlet's dam wants to see you. She isss worried about that wounded wing."

Drakor tried to straighten his body, to look more like a leader. As he moved his leg, it began to bleed through the bandages. "Huh. That dwire bite isss deeper than I thought."

Merika glared. "I warned you to lie still. You were hurt that badly and *still* you had to fight?" Reaching into her Healer bag, she tossed Jardor a roll of bandages and a jar of salve.

He caught them neatly.

"Jardor, you know how to use this. Please change his bandage and keep him still. Drakor, drink the broth." Merika spun on her heel and left the den.

* * *

Jardor flicked his tail while he changed the bandage. "She isss quite angry."

Drakor nodded. "Merika isss a Healer. Because I fought, she had three dragons to heal instead of one."

Jardor tied off the bandage. He turned to Scree and spoke slowly. "I heard you can read dragon jaws. Thank you again for coming so far to help."

Drakor sighed. "You read that conversation?"

Scree nodded and signed, "Merika has good reasons to be angry. She had too many patients with almost no help. You, her mate, were nearly dead. And, have you noticed her wing tips? They're silvery."

Drakor's eyes were huge. "No *wonder* she isss so mad. Merika isss with egg!"

Scree grinned. "Yes. And she's tired of patching you up. This is not a job I seek, either, but I worked too hard on your mangled wing to lose you now."

Scree curled an arm beneath her head, in a dragon's thinking pose. "Hearts are as fascinating as bones. An octopus has one main heart and two small hearts. Fish have one heart with two chambers. But a dragon has one heart with four chambers, all together! It was an interesting challenge to reset a dragon's heart."

Drakor reached out a hand, slowly, and Scree twined arm-to-claw. "I owe you my life, once again. Thank you."

Scree laughed. "I saved your wing the last time, not your life."

Drakor shook his head. "Flying isss life. Scree, you were right. The inner battle was hard."

She signed, "And you won. You let go of your anger."

Jardor raised one eye ridge. "Drakor, when you fought, you kept moving to the east. You knew where that hole was under the snow?"

Drakor nodded. "I memorized the fight circle before it snowed. I knew that hole could be useful. Scree, when you fought three giant squid, you made a hidden hole. It helped you survive that fierce blow. I fought Mardor the same way I did the first time, to throw him off guard, so I could lead him to the hidden hole."

Jardor shook his head. "Drakor, it was risky. Why did you agree to fight?"

Drakor stared out the entrance, where a light snowfall swirled through the afternoon sky. "Mardor knew I was hurt, and still he wanted to fight me. He was healthy, rested, and huge. How could he possibly lose? Mardor wanted to beat me so completely that nobody could question that *he* was the leader."

Drakor flicked the tip of his tail, which was the only part of him that did not hurt. "I could have refused. Or I could have agreed to fight him after my leg healed. But we were already fighting. Mardor challenged my leadership every day; he fought with hidden claws. I had to prove to his followers that *I* am the clan leader, and fights are all they understand. The snow hid the hole, and I knew where it was."

Drakor started coughing.

Jardor offered his flask, and Drakor took a few sips. "Thanks. The whole world was changed by our Volcano. We have a new home. We will face dwire and starving times and problems that I cannot imagine. We need a united clan to survive."

Jardor shook his head. "It was still risky. He could have missed that hole. And you nearly died."

Drakor smiled. "True. Plans seldom work out as we hope, especially with fights. But this was my best chance, when the snow was perfect and Mardor was so confident of winning. Size matters, but a good plan isss stronger."

Jardor cocked his head sideways. "You sound more sure of yourself."

Drakor grinned. "I defeated Mardor *twice*. Everyone knows that *I* am the leader. But we need leaders who can plan, not just beat up another dragon."

Jardor bowed. "You are a good leader."

Drakor nodded. "I am. And I plan to remain the leader. Much has changed, and the clan needs something constant. But, some day, I want to have a new leader for the clan. Then I will be free to explore."

"No ice dragon just stops being leader! Who would be next?"

"You, I hope."

Jardor snapped his tail with a loud crack. "NO. I do not want to fight you."

Drakor looked him in the eye. "I do not want any more challenge fights. I want a new way to choose the leader. We will use the choosing game to decide almost everything I can think of. Ice dragons love making blue fires! Soon, they will *want* to have a choice. Then, when the time isss right, the clan members will choose their new leader."

"Did you plan all this, before you fought?"

Drakor started to shrug his wings and winced. "I never liked challenge fights, but I never considered another way until I met the golden dragons. I challenged Mardor on our island because I knew we had to move. I had to win that fight. I fought here, the second time, to finish the first fight. I did *not* plan to be nearly killed. Jardor, you would be a good leader. You understand what needs to be done and have the patience to deal with the clan every day."

Jardor looked toward the fight circle. "I will think on this. What will you do with Mardor?"

Drakor sighed. "I do not know. I am just one dragon. But change can start with just one dragon."

* * *

Drakor stared at Merika's wings. "When were you going to tell me?"

"What?"

He nodded toward her silvery wingtips. "That."

Merika smiled. "Oh. That. The color began to change the day the dwire attacked. Then *you* were beyond hearing, and *I* was beyond busy."

Drakor ignored the dig about his fight and simply grinned. "Our own dragonlet! Our egg will hatch in summer . . ." He stared out at the snow. "But there will be no spring or summer, only winter."

Merika nodded. "I know. I miss our hot springs. It

213

isss a challenge to nest here, even in summer. It would be nearly impossible in winter. Dorali invited me to nest in their cave."

"You can study with the Healers."

Merika looked south. "Yes. A golden dragon fills her nest bowl with sand. She warms the bowl with dragon-fire, which safely warms the sand and the egg within. But breathing fire on a ceramic bowl does not feel right for an ice dragon."

"What will you do, instead?"

"Make a traditional ice dragon nest using rocks and gems. Our egg will be in sand, like a golden dragon's nest, but I will warm the sand with your new heat-zap. This should feel like the hot springs of our old home."

Drakor gazed at his mate. "That sounds perfect." He clicked his claws together. "We need a place for dragons to nest *here* during this long winter. The clan should build a special den, just for nesting. This would be a safer place even after winter ends and spring finally returns."

Merika's eyes lit up. "Yes!" She brushed off a patch of the dirt floor beside Drakor, making it smoother. Then, using a sharp claw, she began to draw. "The nesting den must be big enough to hold four large dragons. It should be in the safest place, here, in the middle of the village. We must be able to fold the roof, to take it off for the hatching ceremony. The den walls would be thicker, with many layers of rock to keep us warm in winter and cool in summer. They would also be shorter so we can all watch as the egg hatches."

She drew more marks in the floor. "Narrow slits to open during the summer heat and cover in winter. Baskets of river sand will be kept here, with holes for water buckets along this wall."

Drakor ran his eyes over the drawing and nodded. "You thought of everything. When the den isss ready, ice dragons will nest in *our* village. Then we can properly welcome our new dragonlets."

Merika smiled. "This will be a good home. Now you must eat." She turned away and peered into her Healer bag. "Where isss that sea salt? Ah, there." She poured some into the bowl she held. "This has some of the minerals you need to grow more blood."

When she looked away, Drakor stretched his body stealthily, slowly, as slow as a stalking dragon. Then his body spasmed and he gasped, wincing with pain.

Merika whipped her head around. "I warned you to lie still! Your wounds are deeper than you think. If not for Scree . . ." She shuddered, nearly dropping the black onyx bowl that she held. Salty, scented steam rose from within. "You are much too thin. Eat all of this, but slowly. This isss a thicker broth, almost a stew."

Lying still was a new form of torture, but he noted the loose, scaly skin on his body. Drakor studied his reflection in one of the flat, polished sides of Merika's five-sided bowl. He looked like a corpse, and it was not a good look. With all his wounds, he even smelled like something dead.

Drakor tried a spoonful of broth. "Dragon spices!" He finished eating and looked hopefully at the empty bowl.

Merika shook her head. "Not yet. Eating too much, too soon, would hurt you."

Drakor sighed and picked at his blankets. "I broke Mardor's leg. Isss he healing well? Will he be able to push off and fly?"

Merika snorted. "Mardor will recover and have a weather-bone to predict change. The weather isss always snow, so that isss not a very useful talent."

"And the dragonlet? Will she be able to fly?"

Merika gazed in the direction of that den. "I hope so. That wing frame we made isss working even better than I hoped. Her bones are mending. Dorali isss encouraging scales to grow across wounds. She isss painfully aware of her own scars, and pleased that these are harder to see on a white dragon."

Merika gave Drakor a big, steaming mug. "This isss herb tea with honey. Drink all of it."

"My favorite! My throat feels as dry as a mud-cracked stream bed in summer." He finished the tea. The den faded away as he spun down into darkness. His last thought was that she must have added something extra to make him sleep.

*   *   *

Drakor's nose awoke to a new scent. He opened his eyes. Merika was gone.

Arak offered him a steaming bowl. "Have some broth. Merika's worn out, so I offered to watch over you while you both slept."

Drakor said, "Thank you. She needs rest more than I do. I wish I could have won as I planned, without these wounds."

Arak nodded. "It *would* be nice if plans cooperated. I'm glad we were already on our way."

Arak smiled. "We have a good team here. Scree has unique skills. Dorali and Merika take turns micro-zapping injuries. Jardor gets the food supplies, and then Karoon and I fix meals. We all help change bandages. Jordana helps, too."

Drakor flicked his tail. "Jordana isss learning our ways, but she still misses the golden dragons." He gave a sad smile. "We have three wounded, den-bound ice dragons. Before I fought, there was only one. Because of me, we need all of you."

Arak gave Drakor's shoulder a careful, reassuring pat. "This fight was going to happen. I'm glad we could help."

Drakor's lump of guilt began to thaw like ice in spring. "Thank you. How was your trip here?"

"Interesting. We stopped for lunch and spent each night on a beach, so Scree could rest in the surf, and we could warm up by a fire. It's safer by the sea, easier to defend if dwire attack. My favorite is still that pebble beach with the glowing waves."

Drakor's eyes lit up. "That isss one of my favorite places. I will never forget our sea journeys. The skiff became home. Someday . . ."

Arak cocked his head sideways. "You wish to travel again? You'll always be welcome aboard the dragon-skiff."

Zardan crawled in through the narrow entrance, bringing tantalizing aromas that filled the den. He placed a heavy tray on the low table. There were plates of food and a bowl. He handed the bowl to Drakor. "You look better already! Dorali made fish broth with herbs and salts."

Zardan turned to Arak and bowed low. "Thank you again for coming here. These are the new food favorites: smoked redfish, cranberries, toasted nuts, and dried mushrooms."

Arak's stomach rumbled as he eyed the food. The strange, tan mushrooms were hollow, with a honeycomb pattern of ridges and pits. He began eating and thumped his tail. "This is superb!"

Zardan put a plate on the stool next to Scree. This was carved from solid red jasper, polished smooth, with a tall rim to hold the feast within. Ruffled gray oysters, brown clams, and shiny black mussels were arranged in an attractive starburst pattern.

He bowed low. "Thank you for saving my son."

Scree turned happy-green. "You're welcome. You found my favorite foods! Thanks. With the sea so cold, these must be hard to get."

He laughed. "The icy shore makes it a challenge to hunt, and there isss less to find, but you deserve a proper feast."

Night closed in, with auroras dancing in the sky.

Drakor pointed outside. "That sky fire moves faster than smidgers on a warm day. There are colors I have never seen! They remind me of Orm's glowing sea creatures."

Arak gazed at the sky. "When we play games with colored lightning, the clouds glow with rainbow fires. But this is the best light show ever!"

Zardan's eyes glowed. "These are even better than the auroras at our old home. Now I have new legends to share."

Drakor nodded. "These new sky colors are a gift from our Volcano, to welcome us to our new home."

Zardan gazed at his son. "I thought I would lose you. That fight will become a clan legend."

Drakor sighed. "I hope the most memorable part of the story isss that this was the *last* challenge fight."

*   *   *

A five-day passed.

Bright auroras glowed green through the ceiling, adding their light to the flickering candles in Drakor's den. Notes from a flute duet flowed like another layer of warmth.

Ice dragons gathered near the entrance, tapping their claws in the snow, matching the rhythm. Scree held a hollow silver ball between two arms, feeling the vibration patterns.

Merika and Dorali finished the tune and bowed.

Dragons snapped their tails in applause when the tune ended. Scree showed her delight with a rainbow that swirled down each arm. Then her skin became a night sky, with emerald auroras that spread across the stars until she was completely happy-green.

Drakor stared. "Scree, you change colors faster than lightning. How do you think so fast?"

Scree shrugged her octopus-shoulders. "It helps to have nine brains."

Drakor laughed. "I can only imagine." He turned to the dragon-ladies. "That was magnificent. Could you play at the feast?"

Dorali pointed her flute at Drakor. "You should play, too. And Arak. Merika, there's room for all of us to practice in the visitor's den."

Drakor sighed. "Mardor thought that den was a waste of time. Who would visit? But now you're all here, healing three dragons. Thank you again."

Jardor poked his head in. "Merika and Dorali, the

dragonlet needs you again." After they left, he entered the den. Jardor studied his friend and leader, then nodded as if satisfied by the progress. "We caught, cleaned, and smoked five more hands of fish. And we tried Scree's suggestions for dwire warnings."

Drakor's eyes brightened. "What?"

Scree signed, "The dwire camouflage so you can't see them, but sound and smell are also important. We knew that giant squid would attack our pod, so we hung shells on seaweed trees. The shell noise gave us warning. Then we broke stinky, rotten eggs to hide the scent of our octopus fighters."

Jardor took a box out of his sack. "I designed noisy, smelly, warning traps."

Drakor grinned. "What did you use?"

Jardor opened the box. "This thin wood box squashes easily. The dry sticks inside break and make noise. For smell, I added that strange mushroom with orange arms, the one you call stinky squid. Nothing too awful in case a dragon steps on a box."

Jardor looked toward the field. "When it was dark, we hid the boxes under the snow, near the forest. When a box isss stepped on, the noise and smell should warn the guards."

Drakor said, "Guards?"

Jardor nodded. "I added guards. It isss what you would have done, if you could have."

Drakor grinned. "Yes, but you were clever enough to not be unconscious."

CHAPTER 20: DANGEROUS WAVES

Another five-day passed, and Drakor's bruises now showed purple beneath his scales. He glanced at his mate, who had turned away. Then he slowly stretched, reaching his claws toward a long, puckered scar.

Merika spun back. "Do NOT scratch."

"Everything itches."

"Be glad you are alive to feel the itch. Try walking again." She held his elbow firmly, keeping him steady as he sat up and slowly stood.

Jardor appeared at the entrance. He looked Drakor up and down, studying the lighter bandages that no longer bled through. "You can walk?"

Drakor nodded.

"Good. It isss time."

Merika shook her head no. "He nearly died. He needs more time to heal."

Drakor took a step toward the entrance. "Jardor isss right."

Merika walked by his side, holding his elbow. He twisted out of her grip and gently placed both hands on her shoulders, claws back. "Merika, I need to do this alone."

He looked Jardor in the eye. "Thank you for all you have done for me and the clan. Call the meeting, and I will come. But there isss something I must do first." Then he left the den, alone.

Drakor limped away. He winced as he put weight on his left leg, which was still swollen from the dwire's toxic bite. Everything hurt. Finally, he reached Mardor's home.

Drakor stretched taller, feeling each stitch and puckered scar. He nodded to the two dragon guards. "Please move back." Then he entered the dragon's den, alone.

Mardor sat at the far back, beyond sight of curious dragons strolling by. His scales were polished, and the wounds seemed mostly healed. He narrowed his eyes at the unwelcome visitor and growled, "Why are you here?"

Drakor studied Mardor's home in silence. This den was huge, but so was Mardor. It was spartan, nearly empty. There was no glittering hoard of gems, no cache of tasty food, just his chest pouch and a simple bed of leaves. Most dragons had more, even dragonlets! Why did he want so much control, but so little stuff? Was power his only love?

Drakor cocked his head sideways. "Why did you want to be leader? It isss not that much fun."

Mardor's eye ridges rose up in surprise. "You do not want the power? That isss more precious than chocolate."

Drakor gazed back toward the meeting circle. "Isss having power truly worth all the fights?"

Mardor shrugged his wings. "To me, it isss everything. I cannot imagine a different life. And now I will die." There was no anger or hate, as if the fight had washed this away like clean snow.

Drakor sighed. By clan law, he should either kill Mardor or banish him forever. But he was the leader, and this was *his* decision. "Mardor, I will not kill you, and I will not allow the clan to kill you. But you broke our oldest rule. You will be outcast for three moons. When the moon isss full for the third time, you may return."

Mardor snapped his tail in surprise. "Why?"

Drakor looked him in the eye. "Dragons should not kill dragons. There are too few of us already."

Mardor bowed his head. Then he eyed Drakor's bandages. "Letting me live isss more than I would have done for you."

Drakor gave a wry grin. "I know. You wanted me dead. You have wanted this since we fought the first time."

Mardor stared. "You knew. And you did not want *me* dead? You could have killed me with a lightning sword in the fight. You have the skill."

Drakor shrugged his wings. "We are different

223

dragons. But you have been a huge thorn between my scales." He shared a lopsided grin. "As I once was for you."

Mardor gave a rusty smile. Then he stared past Drakor, into the scraggly forest beyond. "I thought I would die. I did not think past my fate. I am disgraced. I can leave, but I do not see how I can return."

Drakor sank down to the ground beside Mardor. He took two precious pieces of chocolate out of his pouch and gave one to his former foe.

Mardor's eyes grew wide, but he accepted the treat. They ate together in silence.

Then Drakor said, "My sire did not want to live when he could not fly. Dying can seem easier than living. But life brings change. You lost two challenge fights. You will not be leader again. But there isss more in life than being the clan leader. You are a strong dragon and a strong fighter. We could use your help if the dwire attack again. You are part of the clan."

Mardor's lip curled back. "YOUR clan."

"No. OUR clan. The clan isss for all of us, not one dragon. Now we must go to the Meeting Circle. The clan isss waiting. I did not want you to walk alone."

Drakor and Mardor walked together, followed by the two guards. Their breath froze in small clouds. New snow muffled their steps and covered the bloody field, as if that terrible fight had never happened. But it had.

Drakor walked to the center of the ring, followed by Mardor. The giant stood tall with stiffly folded wings, but he seemed to have shrunk. Mardor was just a normal dragon facing something beyond his worst nightmares. This must take more courage than anything else he had ever done.

Drakor nodded to Jardor, and he struck the drum once. Thunder rumbled through the air. Drakor raised his wings high, wincing as this pulled on his many stitches. "I won the challenge fight in our old home. I won again in our new home. I Am The Leader."

The entire clan bowed low in unison. They were quieter now and calmer, too. Every dragon seemed to accept Drakor's rule, relieved that the constant conflict was over at last. There was one clear leader.

A dragon-lord raised his wing politely, and Drakor nodded for him to speak. "Mardor used lightning as a weapon in the challenge fight. He should die!"

Another raised his wing. "He broke our oldest rule. He deserves death!"

A low chant of "Death. Death. Death." rose from clusters of dragons. They were like sharks with blood in the water, circling for the kill.

Mardor remained a silent white statue, but his gray eyes flicked around the circles, seeking old cronies. They met his gaze and looked away.

Drakor recalled Scree's warning: *Anger and hate are dangerous waves that build on each other.* He raised his wings for silence, determined to stop this now. "NO. He should not die. Mardor made a mistake. Who has not made a mistake?"

Wings rustled as the crowd grew quiet.

Drakor stood taller. "I am the leader. We need everyone. That dragonlet was helped from his shell because we have no dragons to waste."

Drakor turned to face his former foe. "Mardor, you broke clan law when you used a lightning sword against

225

another dragon. Therefore, you will be outcast for three moons. You will leave at dawn. When the moon isss full for the third time you may return, to be welcomed back."

Drakor turned in a circle, catching every eye. "Mardor has been, and will be, a valued member of our clan."

The giant looked at him in surprise and then bowed low, finally accepting Drakor as the leader.

* * *

The following dawn, Drakor rose early. His breath froze in small white clouds as he walked to Mardor's den, carrying a large, lumpy sack. "Here. This has salve for your wounds and dried fish. It isss a start, and you are a good hunter. I will walk with you into the forest."

Mardor accepted the sack with a silent bow. He donned his chest pouch and pulled the blanket off his bed of leaves.

Drakor eyed the blanket, which was rough and plain, woven from uneven strips of hemp. In fact, it was ugly. Mardor did not seem to care about any possessions, only power. Now he was disgraced, powerless, and alone. Would he return, or disappear like the morning mist?

They walked together in silence, heading north, until they were hidden by the frost-covered bushes and stunted trees. There, on the ground, two dark branches made a "V" against the snow.

Drakor pointed northwest. "There isss a small cave at the base of the hill, hidden behind a bush. I found it when I was exploring. This isss my private cave, but you need it now. It isss too cold to be without shelter. This trail of sticks leads to the cave. Toss the sticks away as you find them, so no one can follow."

Mardor studied Drakor as if truly seeing him for the first time, as a fellow dragon. "Thank you. This isss more than I deserve."

Drakor shook his head no. "A small octopus once taught me that everyone deserves consideration. I was hungry, so I tried to kill her. She stopped me cold, knocked me out, and then healed my broken wing. She gave me back the sky! I asked her why, and she said, 'I could have killed you. But a live friend isss worth more than a dead enemy.'"

"That isss Scree? She *stopped* you?"

"Yes."

"And now you are friends."

"Yes."

Mardor dropped his blanket and sack in the snow. He put out his hands, claws back.

Drakor smiled and met his hands, claws back. "I will see you in three moons. Then you can help me lead the defense against the dwire."

Mardor smiled back. "Yes." He picked up the sack and blanket, then headed for the secret cave with a new spring in his step.

*   *   *

Glittering flecks of ice spun in the air, glowing like crystal fireflies. This whirling cloud was just above the snow, sparkling like an earthbound aurora. Drakor watched the whirlwind until it fell apart. More weird weather, but this was beautiful and harmless.

He inhaled slowly, noting the scents of fish, clams, mushrooms, cranberries, lichens, nuts, and chocolate! Bright gemstone jars held root-beer, a New World favorite made with sassafras tree roots. This would be a meal to remember, a proper farewell feast for their visitors.

Drakor looked toward the shore with a sad smile. It was even colder now, and Arak was not willing to risk Scree on a return flight through the frozen clouds. Instead, the dragon-skiff had arrived to bring the visitors home, and Merika. They would all leave at dawn.

BROOOM! BROOOM! BROOOM! The drum thundered three times, rumbling through the air.

Dragons dropped everything and headed for the feasting table. Youngsters began snapping their tails and others joined in, united by the catchy rhythm. This spread through the clan like a northern wind, and the cheerful sound rang across the snow.

A dragon-lady scooped up a clawfull of snow, warmed it with a zap from her claws, and threw the slush ball at her suitor. It slid comically off his face. Soon the snow was flying like a winter storm.

Jardor clouted Drakor on the back, gently. "This isss fun. I cannot imagine such foolishness with Mardor as leader."

Drakor nodded. "The clan isss pleased that the conflict isss finally settled. Now we have just one leader."

Jardor shook his head. "That isss only part of it. You are a different sort of leader. No one *wants* to challenge you."

Drakor laughed. "Isss that because they like me as leader, or because they have lost interest in being sliced up? If any dragon challenged me now, he could win the fight. But I hope there will never be another challenge fight."

Jardor raised an eye ridge. "This isss one of our

oldest customs. Do you really think you can change it?"

Drakor looked down at his abundant stitches and scars. Sometimes they itched so fiercely he wanted to shred his scales with scratching. "Yes. And we must. Arak says that everything worth doing starts with a dream."

Jardor nodded. "Ending the challenge fights isss a worthy dream."

Drakor gazed at the table. "And this isss a worthy feast. We should fill extra plates for the visitors on the skiff."

Jardor pointed to a large tub in the meeting circle. "I finished this just in time. Now Scree and Orm can both join the fun."

Drakor walked over and touched the water. "Good. It isss warm. Orm brought food to help us through the winter."

Jardor's eyes grew wide. "Remember when I asked 'How can an octopus help a dragon'? I never imagined a tiny, boneless creature could be so helpful."

Drakor laughed. "Size isss not everything."

*   *   *

Scree relaxed in her tub on the skiff. "The dragons built a special basin just for us, so we can enjoy the celebration."

Orm looked toward the distant gathering. "Terrific. Now I can finally sit in the middle of a horde of ice dragons. Another dream come true."

Scree twined arms with her mate, carefully. "Drakor is the leader, and he's made it clear that we're honored guests."

Orm shrugged. "But will they all listen? Remember the first time you met him? He attacked, and you knocked him out. Six of my arms have toxic tips, just in case."

Just then, Drakor landed right beside them. He held out a colorful stone blade. "Scree, I carved this surgeon's knife from a new Volcano rock."

The round handle flattened into a thin blade. Bands of color flowed across the stone like waves washing onto the shore: maroon, amethyst, red-violet, golden tan, and blue-gray. This was an Earth rainbow with the feel of the sea.

Scree felt the edge, and her eyes glowed. "Thank you. It's beautiful! The edge is knapped so thin it's as clear as ice. This is the sharpest knife I've ever felt!" She placed the blade between two long shells and slipped this into her Healer bag.

Drakor beamed. "Then it isss perfect for the sharpest Healer I have ever known."

Scree and Orm squished into their flying suits, climbed onto Drakor's back, and settled between his wings. He flew them to the gathering, and they slid off into the large, sea-filled basin.

Scree gazed at the crowd of dragons with interest while Orm, with equal interest, rechecked the toxic tips in his arms. Scree grabbed one of his safe arms. "Orm, look!"

The sunset glowed with raging reds and fiery golds. Glittering ice covered the sea of snow, reflecting these colors, surrounding the festival with a vivid display of fire. Then the sun disappeared. Red and green auroras sparkled against the darkness, transforming the night sky into precious black opal.

As Orm gazed at the sky, his stiff arms began to relax. "I *must* find a way to create undersea auroras."

Drakor signed, "And I must see the glowing tapestries in your den." He nodded to Jardor, and the signal drum thundered.

The entire crowd became silent.

Drakor raised his wings high. "We feasted on the gifts of our New World to honor those who flew so far to help us: Arak, Dorali, Karoon, and Scree." He bowed to each as he spoke. "Now, Dorali will share the unique art of golden dragons."

Dorali walked to the center and held up an amber snowflake. It glowed in the firelight, like a frost-covered spider web reflecting the dawn.

Ice dragons leaned forward with wide eyes, snapping their tails in appreciation.

Dorali smiled. "This is an ornament for our winter solstice tree. Dragon-ladies grow fancy snowflakes in the winter clouds, using trace metals and micro-zaps. We place the snowflake on liquid pine sap, zap to turn it to amber, and cut out the design."

She held up more amber flakes. One had a design of leaping fish, another had dragons.

A dragon-lady raised her wing. "Could we learn this art?"

Dorali grinned. "Yes."

Drakor raised his wings, and everyone fell silent. "Thank you, Dorali. We could plan a united dragon festival with games and cloud art. Now we will hear the music of flutes."

Four golden dragons moved to the center of the meeting circle. Drakor pulled out his flute and joined them.

At a signal, Arak, Taron, and Drakor played the flute

melody. Karoon added a sparkling clash of cymbals, their new metal instrument. Then Dorali joined in with a flute harmony that soared and dove like a playful dragon. Bright notes spilled across the moonlit snow.

The audience stood perfectly still, ears tilted forward, entranced.

Drakor relaxed into the music as he played. Everything was working out. Then he noticed odd shadows at the edge of the forest that did not match the trees. Dwire!

He caught Jardor's attention and pointed an elbow toward the shadows. His second-in-command took a closer look and nodded, adding their sign for dwire. Drakor continued playing the flute while Jardor quietly spoke to dragons.

The following dawn, Drakor stood on the skiff, wishing the guests farewell. Extra guards had watched through the night, and the dwire had not attacked. As the skiff rocked beneath him, he felt the pull of the sea, like a tide drawing him back.

Last of all, Drakor bid farewell to Merika. "I will mind-call."

Merika met his hands. "I will be waiting."

Drakor flew ashore and watched until the skiff disappeared beyond the tantalizing horizon. He resisted the urge to fly high and watch longer. At least their egg would be in the warmer, well-protected cave of golden dragons. He sighed and turned away. There was work to do.

Ice dragons flew back to their village, carrying the plates and remaining food.

As the sun set, Drakor flew high above the fields,

searching for dwire. He found monstrous dark shadows that rippled across the snow, ten times larger than the dragons who made them. Ice dragons were nearly invisible on snow but, as the sun sank, their shadows grew enormous in the slanting light.

He imagined monstrous dwire shadows and shuddered. Were these hunters gathered just inside the forest, hiding their shadows, watching and waiting?

CHAPTER 21: FRACTURED ICE

An eerie wind moaned outside. Drakor sat on the floor of his den, carving a bowl from the new Volcano gem: black ice. He smoothed off the last rough edge and held it up to the candle light. The glassy bowl was clear darkness, like a solid night sky. Black ice was the perfect name.

Drakor set the bowl down and fixed a mug of tea. He inhaled the spicy steam and swallowed it down, warming himself from within.

Merika had mind-called. Their egg was a large, healthy size. She was learning the Healer micro-zaps. And the last of the golden dragons would soon arrive, completing their move to the New World. Then they would have a clan-and-pod festival with dragons and octopi.

Drakor clicked his claws together. After the festival, Scree and Orm would leave to follow the route of the disappearing fish. He hoped Arak could use his secret gift to keep an eye on them as they skiff-flew.

Drakor looked toward their ice-covered lake. It seemed that these fish were also leaving, swimming down the river to the sea. Would they return? If not, the ice dragons had a new, serious problem. If Scree learned what was happening, the clan would need to help fix it. She was right: everything was connected.

Drakor moved to the entrance, pushed the blanket aside, and poked his head out. He took a deep, frozen breath. As he exhaled, sparkling frost grew on his scales. When would this winter end?

Thick clouds covered the moon and stars, making the night even darker than the bowl he carved. Drakor stepped outside, crunching through the icy crust. He stared into the darkness, toward his secret cave in the forest, flicking his tail nervously. This was the third full moon since Mardor left. He should be back.

Mardor had served his time in exile. This was the lightest sentence Drakor could give, a careful balance between consequences and concern for a dragon. With a sheltering cave and a lake for fishing, he should have survived. Had the dwire found him? Even the most ferocious dragon could die in an ambush, unable to reach the safety of the sky or the help of the clan. Was he hurt? Or worse?

Where was Mardor?

Drakor stared into the night, trying to pierce the darkness. If that dragon did not return soon, he and Jardor would search . . .

A powerful roar shook the sky.

That was a dragon! Drakor was in the air before he knew it, gathering energy with his claws. He whistled a piercing warning to the clan as he flew.

The wind grew, tearing at the sky. Moonlight bled through a tattered patch of clouds. At the edge of the field, a huge dragon spun on the snow, claws flying, battling an invisible whirlwind.

Drakor hovered in the sky just above the dragon, working his wings to hold still. He threw lightning swords with both hands, striking the nearly invisible attackers, creating a perfect ring of death around Mardor.

Dwire shrieked in rage and pain. As the dwire died, their chameleon hides became visible, a mottled gray-brown. But even in death, they clung to the dragon like leeches in a swamp. As the dragon was pulled down, more dwire leapt for his throat.

Drakor killed the last clinging dwire just as Mardor collapsed on the battlefield.

More dragons appeared in the sky, throwing lightning swords. The invisible dwire were betrayed by their faint shadows. There were many tens of dwire!

Drakor landed beside the massive, shredded dragon that lay bleeding in the snow. Mardor's perfect, sparkling white scales were now sliced, shredded, and scarlet.

Mardor whispered, "You came when I called."

Drakor nodded. "Of course. You are part of the clan."

Mardor stared at the dead attackers. Some dwire still clung to his hide, with their jaws clenched in death. There were rings of burnt dwire all around him, yet no burn had touched the dragon in the middle. This was the work of a lightning artist. "You always were better with lightning swords." His eyes rolled up in his head, and his body went limp.

Drakor called to his in-commands. "Cranart, check the village for dwire. Tenira, get a toboggan, four helpers, and blankets. Take Mardor to his den as fast as you can and keep him warm."

Drakor scanned the snow. The field was littered with death, but still there were fresh tracks leading from the battle into the forest. How many dwire were there? He pried open the jaws of dead dwire and removed them from Mardor's body. Chunks of flesh had been ripped out, and blood ran freely.

Drakor burned with anger. He flung the dead dwire as far away as he could, calming down as he cleared a path for the toboggan. If not for Mardor's warning . . . He gathered clean snow and began washing the wounds of the scarlet giant.

Five dragons arrived and stared at the bloody giant. They carefully slid Mardor onto the toboggan and tied his limp wings to his body, but his feet and tail trailed beyond. The dragons covered him with blankets, grabbed the toboggan ropes, and pulled, picking up speed as they moved across the snow.

Drakor turned to Jardor. "The dwire planned this attack well. They need to hide their shadows, yet they chose a night with a full moon, a time we would least expect. They waited for thick clouds, for the darkest night with a moon. They even avoided our sound traps . . . they must have watched us place them!"

237

Jardor snapped his tail. "We need a new plan."

Drakor nodded. "Yes. Please take over here while I help Mardor."

Jardor nodded toward the bloody trail in the snow. "Isss there hope?"

Drakor gazed up at a star that escaped from the clouds. "The stars will decide, but Mardor isss the toughest dragon I know."

Jardor shook his head. "No. Mardor isss the second toughest dragon. You are tougher. Go do what you can."

Drakor's eyes widened in surprise. Then he nodded to Jardor and leapt into the sky. He flew to his den and grabbed his Healer bag. He tossed journey food into his pouch and slung it over one shoulder. He flung his blanket over the other shoulder, picked up another bag, and sprinted for Mardor's den.

Drakor reviewed Healer lessons from his skiff journeys with Scree and Dorali, and from Merika's classes. He knew the basics and more, but would this be enough? And his Healer bag felt rather thin, barely adequate. What would he give for Merika's well-stocked bag?

Drakor reached Mardor's den just as the unconscious giant arrived on the toboggan. He helped push this into the den. Then he dropped his own stuff by the wall. "Tenira, could you stay?" He pointed to another dragon. "Ask Jordana to come, and walk with her. Dwire could still be lurking in the shadows. Then I need one of you to wait outside this den, to help. Take turns waiting here or helping Jardor."

Drakor and Tenira stood on opposite sides of Mardor, working as fast as they could. Blood continued to drip onto the floor and seep into the dirt. An aroma of death filled the air, mixed with earthy scents of herbs and moss.

Tenira cleaned a deep cut and pushed in peat moss. "He isss so big, and there are so many wounds! How can we stop all the bleeding in time?"

Drakor wrapped another bandage. "Cold snow and peat moss will help slow the bleeding until we can treat all of his wounds. But how much blood can he lose, and still live?"

Tenira paused, took out her water flask, and drank it down. "Why did you ask for Jordana? She isss so young she cannot even fly."

Drakor tied a knot in the bandage. "She has as much Healer experience as I do and, being so young, isss small enough to squeeze into the den with us."

Tenira nodded toward Drakor's pile of stuff. "And the blanket?"

Drakor tied another bandage knot. "Mardor needs someone to stay with him."

She smiled. "You would be best for that."

Drakor placed his claws over each wound and zapped as he worked, using up his own inner energy to help Mardor live. This was the fastest way to stop bleeding and speed healing. But there were so many wounds! Soon his hands trembled and his scales felt gray.

Tenira looked over at Drakor and snapped her tail with a loud crack. "You must save some of your own energy." She tossed him a pouch of walnuts, and he barely caught it. "Take a break. Eat this and drink some water."

Drakor fumbled to open the pouch. He studied the floor as he ate, quietly fuming. After all he had accomplished, he felt like a dragonlet being reprimanded.

Tenira must have noticed. "I apologize. I should have said that differently, but you looked so drained that it scared me. You are still healing from a near-fatal wound. Merika needs you, and so does the clan."

Drakor squared his wings, trying to look energetic. "You were right. I need to pace myself. We still have wounds to clean and bandage. Sometimes I feel . . ." He paused. "I am the smallest leader the clan ever had. Mardor isss huge. He always *looked* like the perfect leader, perfectly groomed and in control."

Tenira bowed. "Nobody questions your size. Maybe your common sense . . ." She laughed. "What *sane* dragon would want to fight Mardor *twice*? And you were right about our Volcano."

His eyes grew wide. "You knew?"

She nodded. "I knew the legends and the signs, but where would we go? Then you found a place. When Mardor would not listen, you beat him. Twice! He isss *not* perfect, and he lost control in that last challenge fight."

"Yes, he did, and paid a price. I hope that price does not include his life."

Tenira studied their patient. "Mardor's warning was timely. He redeemed himself. And even you, the leader, are doing all you can to save him."

Drakor shrugged his wings. "Mardor needs help, and he isss a member of our clan."

"You understand what matters. That isss why *you* are the leader we need."

Jordana entered the den, flicking her tail nervously. The youngster bowed to Drakor. Then she stared at Mardor. His terrible wounds looked even worse in the flickering candlelight. She set her apprentice Healer bag down and, without a word, began working on his bleeding, shredded legs.

Drakor nodded to Jordana as she dripped honey into a deeper wound. "Thank you for coming. We need the help of another Healer."

Jordana smiled shyly and kept working.

Tenira stitched up a section of scaly skin that hung loose, partly ripped away. "I wish Merika was here. She makes better stitches."

Drakor held a long cut together as he stitched. "We could really use her help. It isss hard to match the scales together and make small, even stitches. Mardor has lost so much blood! And how much poison isss in all of these bites? How well does this new salve protect against it? How will we get enough medicine into Mardor, when he isss not even conscious?"

Tenira looked up. "Spoken like a Healer."

Drakor gave a half smile. "I finally understand why Merika was so mad when she had three dragons to heal."

Tenira ran her eyes over the huge patient. "Treating Mardor isss like working on three dragons. We need to turn him over, to reach his other wounds."

Another dragon helped turn him.

Drakor, Tenira, and Jordana continued working. Hours later, their wings hung limp. They were stained with all the shades of blood: bright scarlet, dull burgundy, and a blackish maroon.

Drakor called a halt. "Thank you. We stopped most of the blood loss, and can work on the healing tomorrow."

Jordana bowed. "Thank you for letting me help."

Drakor smiled at the youngster. "You are a Healer,

and we needed your help."

Tenira bowed. "I will walk Jordana home and send another of Merika's students to help, at dawn." Then they both left.

Mardor lay in deathly stillness, barely breathing. Beneath the blankets, he was covered with bandages, mustard-yellow salve, and stitches. The dirt floor around him was muddy-red, soaked with blood, and the stench was overwhelming. Drakor noticed the silence with a fleeting smile. This was an unexpected benefit of the eternal winter: there were no annoying, buzzing flies drawn to the gory feast.

Drakor recalled his recent challenge fight with Mardor, when his own blood was flowing away. Creeping cold had spread through his body before he collapsed into darkness. Mardor must have this same bone-deep cold, since there was not enough blood left to warm him.

Drakor placed the claws of both hands over Mardor's massive, battered chest and zapped healing energy into the heart. The beat grew a little stronger. Then he piled more blankets around his former foe.

Drakor shivered. It was bitterly cold outside and not much better in the den. He washed his hands in a bucket of melted snow, opened his other bag, and took out the bowls filled with quartz crystals. He placed the bowls in a circle around Mardor and touched the crystals with his heat-zap.

Flecks of red glowed inside the hot, clear quartz. These crystals seemed to shimmer as they heated the air, covering the dragon with velvety warmth.

Crystal fire was Drakor's newest discovery, another way to help the clan survive this bitter winter. It was a safe, easy way to warm the den, like adding a stack of weightless blankets. Quartz crystals were everywhere, and they could even be spotted in the ground beneath the snow. Their subtle electric energy drew the inner eye.

Drakor was too weary to polish his scales, but he remembered Tenira's warning and ate a quick snack. He found a fairly clean patch of floor near the back wall, rolled up in his blanket, and immediately dropped into an exhausted sleep.

*   *   *

Drakor opened one eye to a ceiling that glowed orange. The bloody stench told him where he was. Sleep tugged at his eyelids, but he forced himself up to check on the patient.

Mardor was barely breathing. Then he saw the floor by the light of dawn: it was soaked with blood. Had the giant lost too much blood?

Drakor grabbed his bag. Where was the sea salt? Merika had added a few items before she left, but his Healer bag was still rather thin. He mixed a blood-building potion with water, salt, molasses for blood iron, honey for energy, and willow bark extract for swelling and pain. Then he warmed this with a heat-zap.

A dragon-dam entered the den, one of Merika's students. She bowed respectfully to Drakor, but her eyes grew wide. Was she surprised by his unpolished appearance? Or because he was here, helping, unlike a normal leader?

"Thank you for coming. Could you drip this under his tongue, near the back? Drip slowly, one drop at a time, and stop if he coughs."

Jardor poked his head into the den. "Drakor, we need

your decisions."

Drakor nodded. He crawled outside and stared. His blood-stained scales looked even worse in the light. He wrinkled his nose. The den had an overpowering stench, drowning other odors. But now he knew that he, too, smelled terrible.

Drakor grabbed two generous clawfulls of snow and scrubbed his scales until they gleamed. This crystalline cold woke him up completely.

Jardor handed him a steaming mug of tea. "You need this." He tilted his head toward the den. "With so many stitches, Mardor looks like fractured ice. Will he live?"

Drakor finished the tea. "That isss still up to the stars, and Mardor."

Jardor smiled. "And to you. I saw you give Mardor a bag when he left the clan, and there was a trail of sticks in the snow. To a shelter? You gave him a better chance to survive as an outcast. Now you are helping him survive this attack."

Drakor shrugged his wings. "He isss a member of our clan. We need him."

"True. I did not think there could be so many dwire left, after that first attack! What happens now?"

CHAPTER 22: DRAGON DREAMER

Another day passed, and the patient was still unconscious. The dragon-ladies went home for the night, leaving Drakor alone with the wounded giant. Most of the blood-soaked floor had been replaced with new sand, but the odors lingered.

Drakor took shallow breaths, trying to ignore the stench. He carefully wiped off a row of stitches, checking to be sure there was no infection under the dried blood.

Suddenly, the giant opened his eyes and spread his claws, ready to attack.

Drakor backed away. "Mardor. The dwire are gone. You are in your den."

Mardor turned his wild eyes toward the voice. Then he whispered, "Dray--kor."

Drakor's ears twitched; Mardor's voice was impossibly weak. He gave him a water flask. "Drink slowly."

Mardor drained it. "I do not remember ever being this thirsty."

Drakor nodded. "I know exactly how that feels." He smiled. "When I said you could help lead the defense against the dwire, I did not mean you should fight the whole pack by yourself."

Mardor gave a rueful smile. "That was not my plan."

"What happened?"

"I was coming back, walking just inside the forest. Clouds covered the night sky, so I saw no shadows. I heard a crunch. Then the moon escaped from the clouds. There were many tens of hunting shadows sliding across the snow. The dwire spotted me before I was safely up in the sky. I shouted a warning as they pulled me down."

"Your warning saved dragons."

"Good." Mardor looked down at his bandaged body. "I was furious when you marked me. Now, the dwire have marked me so completely that my neck scars no longer matter. You were right, there isss more to life than being the leader. I had three moons to find a new way to live."

Drakor cocked his head sideways. "And?"

"I explored." Mardor reached for his shredded chest pouch, grinning as he pulled out a red opal scale.

Drakor stared. "Sunset dragons! Finally! Where?"

"Southwest. The ground was torn up and smelled of

blood. There were tracks of many dwire but just one dragon, and it was even smaller than you." He ran his eyes across his huge, torn, bandaged body. "Dwire are fierce fighters. How could one small dragon win?"

Drakor looked Mardor in the eye. "Size isss not everything." He clicked his claws together. "According to our legends, sunset dragons are dream-walkers. They can mind-walk with other dragons. Maybe they can also hear dwire minds?"

Mardor stretched slowly, stifling a groan. "A warning would help. If they can sense minds, they know we are here and avoid us. Can sunset dragons stun a mind when they mind-walk?"

Drakor snapped his tail. "Mind-stun? If so, these are deadly dreamers. The sunset dragons may not want to meet us, and they could be dangerous. But I have dreamed of meeting them."

Mardor shook with laughter and winced at the pain. "Have you no fear?"

Drakor looked down at his scars. "Clearly not enough."

Mardor eyed Drakor's abundant scars and grinned. "That isss true. Wait 'til I am well and I will help you search."

Drakor gazed southwest and his smile grew. "Then we will finally meet these mysterious sunset dragons."

SCIENCE & FANTASY TERMS

Abalone – This sea animal can grow to the size of two human hands, with a thick shell. The inside is colorful mother-of-pearl with overlapping layers of silvery pink, green and blue.

Bioluminescent – Life that glows in the dark, making its own light. Fireflies, some fungi (including mushrooms), and many sea creatures are bioluminescent.

Cloth-of-gold – This is real. The fabric is thin, strong, and woven from the wiry roots of the pen shell.

Dam – A dragon's mother. Arafine is Arak's dam.

Dweer – These lived in the old world, in the land of golden dragons: scaly, rust-colored, and about the size of a wolf. A pack attacked and nearly killed Dorali.

Dwire – These scaly creatures live in the New World and have short, stunted wings. They're the size of huge wolves and can change colors to camouflage. A group can attack dragons.

Giant squid – These intelligent predators have eight long arms and two extra-long arms. They live in the deep ocean and can grow up to forty-three feet long. Giant squid have huge eyes, up to twelve inches across.

Lodestone – This iron-rich stone is a natural magnet.

Mantis Shrimp – This predator shrimp uses its claw as a club or spear. Mantis can see and use light beyond our visible spectrum. Some types mate for life, share the same burrow, and can live twenty years.

Octopi – This fits the Dragon Dreamer world better than the term "octopuses"

Pod – Author's term for an octopus group.

Quithra – Imaginary sea creature similar to a sea slug. (kwih-thrah)

Sire – A dragon's father. Zardan is Drakor's sire.

Spartan – To live in a sparse, simple way.

Spawn – When fish release eggs into the water.

Star-stone – Some metal meteorites have high levels of nickel and cobalt. This is similar to stainless steel. A 3,000-year-old dagger found in King Tut's tomb was made from meteorite metal, and it had not rusted.

Strike – Scree's mantis shrimp friend.

Toboggan – Long sled with no runners, pulled across snow with a rope, or used to slide down hills.

Zircon – This rock is found in many colors. Green zircon has radioactive elements that help give it this color.

Words can be beautiful and powerful:

"The pen is mightier than the sword(fish)."
Swordfish meet like the dipping point of an inkwell pen.

AUTHOR'S NOTE

Dragons are large, intelligent beings. The golden dragons love festivals, growing fantasy snowflakes, and playing games with colored lightning. They learn to breathe fire, talk mind-to-mind, and manipulate energy. Ice dragons are even bigger. They enjoy feasts and Winter Games with Slam, Lightning Swords, and Lightning Sculptures. All dragons have ancient traditions and legends.

An octopus is curious, clever, and smaller than dragons. Some types can change colors to show emotion and are natural shape-shifters. The mimic octopus can "assume the form and coloration of at least fifteen other species, including crabs, stingrays, and jellyfish." (Time's Living Wonders book, 2008).

If octopuses choose to mimic other creatures so realistically, they might choose to make skin pictures with their color cells. Especially to talk to dragons.

The octopus life cycle in the Dragon Dreamer world is different from this cycle on Earth, but their abilities to shape-shift, change colors, problem-solve, and create gardens remain the same. Two octopus villages were discovered *after* the first Dragon Dreamer book was published!

ABOUT THE AUTHOR

J.S. Burke has worked as an author, artist, and marine biologist, studying creatures of the dark abyss and diving on coral reefs. Burke lives in Georgia with family, rescue pets, and dragons!

WEBSITE: www.JennySBurke.com

The award-winning Dragon Dreamer series is Science Fantasy with dragons and an undersea world, for young adults 9 to 99.

The Dragon Dreamer (stand-alone book I) won IAN (Book of the Year) First Place for Best First Novel. It's also an IAN Finalist for Best Fantasy and for Best Science Fiction.

Dragon Lightning (stand-alone book II) won Pinnacle First Place for Best Science Fantasy and IAN (Book of the Year) First Place for Best Science Fiction. It's also an IAN Finalist for Best Fantasy and for Best Young Adult book.

Dragon Thunder is stand-alone book III. If you enjoyed this book, could you please leave a rating or a sentence of review on Amazon, Goodreads, or another site? Thank you! Please check out the other books!

This snowflake is made of seals and kelp seaweed, because everyone needs a

"Seal of Approval"

Made in the USA
Columbia, SC
06 December 2022

72823258R00157